The Kersey Cottage

By

Carol Sue Ravenel

To Mary + Eric —
dream and write,
Read and soar!
Traveling on —
Carol
15 October 02

This book is a work of fiction. Places, events, and situations in this story are purely fictional. Any resemblance to actual persons, living or dead, is coincidental.

ISBN: 1-4033-1567-1 (e-book)
ISBN: 1-4033-1568-X (Paperback)

This book is printed on acid free paper.

1st Books - rev. 07/16/02

ACKNOWLEDGEMENT

My sincere gratitude and appreciation for mentoring, support, and editorial considerations to Joyce Christmas, the late Sid Davis, Donna Knoell, Jim Royer, and Hank Searls. To my family, especially my husband Jim, and friends who gave me encouragement to write. And, most importantly, to God who gives me the talent and desire to put stories on paper.

CHAPTER ONE
THE KERSEY COTTAGE

THE REALIZATION… that she was now all alone fell on her heart like a heavy stone. Patti Hopkins, fifteen, and the only child of Cassie and John Hopkins, walked slowly away from the fresh grave site in Evergreen Cemetery.

Patti's parents, so young and eager to make a better life for her, had perished in a car accident on their way home from their menial jobs in downtown Cleveland. Near dusk on that chilly day, Cassie and John were discussing how they could afford a summer vacation. "I'll try to pick up some more overtime," John offered.

"And I can probably find some more alterations work from the women at the warehouse next to mine," Cassie added.

At the corner of St. Clair and 18th Street a pickup truck, driven by an eighteen-year-old known drug dealer, careened into the intersection, through the stop sign, and slammed into their aging station wagon. Despite efforts of the emergency medical teams, neither of them could be revived. John's blow to his head was instant death. The medical team said Cassie also died immediately as a result of the impact. The driver of the truck stood beside his truck in a stupor, watching as if this were just another day in the neighborhood.

1

A small trickle of blood ran down his cheek. His truck barely showed effects of the crash.

****

Cassie was a clerk for a large fabric warehouse and occasionally did some janitorial work for extra pay. John was on the line at a tire producing plant and worked as many extra hours as possible to help save for Patti's intended college and the small house they were buying in an intown neighborhood. It was not the safest place to live in Cleveland, but it was the best they could do given their incomes and their plans for Patti. Surrounded by Willow Freeway, the Inner Belt, and a large municipal parking lot, Woodland Heights was a far comparison to the opulent Shaker Heights in the southeast part of town. They were fully aware of the risks and dangers involved in living inner city, but Patti had "street smarts" and had always been a mindful child. She found jobs after school to help and did her chores at home. In addition to all this, she maintained excellent grades and was assured by her teachers that she would have no trouble getting a scholarship to a fine school. Most of her spare time was spent reading art literature books or taking the bus to any museum that was offering free exhibits... her favorites being the Victorian artists who painted English life.

This gloomy day at the cemetery, with rain and snow, she stood wondering if she would even get to finish high school now that her parents were gone. If only she had had brothers or sisters to share the grief. Her mother's fragility, mixed with a strange chemical imbalance, prompted the doctors to caution her against another pregnancy. Carrying Patti had not been easy for Cassie. She was plagued by nausea, dizziness, and headaches for the entire nine months. The absence of siblings did not seem to affect Patti's emotions. She always found pleasure in dolls, books, maps and anything that could feed her hunger for art and creating. And, there were always children of her age in the neighborhood to whom she could reach out for play.

Cassie and John were very loving parents and constantly encouraged her to succeed, but now who would be there to laugh with her, to give her a warm hug, to chastise when needed, to praise the good grades, to help with braiding that long blond hair into the crown that had become her own special look… "oh, how she would miss them both." Though their lives had been lived simply, if not frugally, she always cherished the peace and serenity that prevailed at home.

Home… it was just a little two-bedroom frame house built on a barren plot of ground not far from the worst sections of Cleveland. John had always been handy and eagerly engaged in painting, repairing cracks, planting trees, and making their little piece of heaven on earth just that… at least that's what it seemed like to Cassie and Patti. He'd put on a fresh coat of white paint, green shutters and patched the leaky roof. Cassie had a window over her kitchen sink where she could watch Patti playing with her dolls and John digging up still another space for his vegetable garden. Summer evenings, when the days were long, they would take walks into Public Square and watch the tourists checking into the Stouffer Inn on The Square, a big, old hotel with an imposing lobby and a man who played the piano right out there in the middle of the lobby lounge. Patti was fascinated with this and tried to see him through the windows, while at the same time straining to hear a bit of his music.

One Saturday afternoon John said he had a special surprise for Cassie and Patti. "Put on your prettiest dresses, ladies, and get into the car. We're going for a surprise ride."

He drove south, passing Garfield Heights, Parma and Seven Hills. At Route 303 he turned west on Route 176 and then to Front Street in the little community of Richfield. Slowly the car eased into the pebbled parking lot of the Taverne of Richfield. Built in 1886, and long known as a social club of the region, it hosted famous people like wealthy John D. Rockefellar, who took delight-pressing coins into the hands of poor children in Richfield. Cassie and Patti were filled with awe and anticipation as they climbed the old wooden stairs to the porch of this lovely old mansion of a bygone era. Looking up from the bottom step, Patti could see the *widow's walk*, which was in reality only a former fence from a pigsty. It did however give character to the strange pitch of the roof. Inside the foyer, a lady in a black jumper and whose white hair was pulled into a severe knot on the back of her head greeted them.

"Good afternoon, may I seat you for dinner?" she asked as John proudly slipped one arm through Cassie's and the other through Patti's. They followed the hostess, looking in awe at every detail of this wonderful mansion.

Patti had never been in a room of such grandeur. The burled walnut mirror and the tulip bracket lamps on either side of the mantle caused her to stare and then her eyes were drawn to the embossed tin ceiling, traditional in Victorian homes of the area. The dining room had beautiful oak tables and a pillared sideboard that she noticed was laden with inviting desserts, which she hoped, would be part of the surprise. The antique brass chandelier once lit with candles, now gave their glow from electricity. Sepia-toned reproductions of life in Richfield lined the walls and kept Patti so engrossed she hardly heard the hostess ask if she were hungry.

The menu, well done in hand-lettered script, listed food that Patti could not pronounce, let alone know what they were. Such things as *Gigot d'Agneau, Chateaubriand a la Bernaise,* and *Foie de Veau,* made her giggle and whisper to her mother. "Do you think they have any hamburgers or chicken noodle soup?" Daddy came to the rescue and said they were going to enjoy a fine steak with all the trimmings, including some of those luscious desserts. Cassie could only wonder where he had found the money for this very extravagant adventure.

All the way home Patti kept thinking, "Someday I'll dine like this on a regular basis." But she did hope they would find some original art for the walls before she returned. As they turned on to Woodlawn, and just as Patti's eyes were about to close, John made a profound statement to Cassie.

"Cass, my love, for about two years I have had a special secret. On those Saturday mornings when you thought I was going out to get a paper and a coffee with the guys, I was really heading to the Emergency Room at St. Vincent's." St. Vincent's was the hospital a few blocks from their house. "I was giving blood, and though they usually take it as a donation, mine has some special antibodies they need, so they were giving me ten dollars each time I came in. Guess we could have used it for the house or Patti's fund, but gosh, we have to have a little slice of life once in a while."

He had tears in his eyes as he turned off the ignition and stumbled out of the car. Cassie fairly flew around the back of the car and threw her arms around him.

"Oh, you dear sweet man. We loved every thing about this day. Didn't we, Patti?", she asked as she kissed him on the cheek.

"Oh yes, Daddy, I will always remember this day as our very specialest!"

As Patti grew into a tall and willowy girl, Cassie realized she needed a special place all her own. To add to the income, Cassie had taken in alterations work from some of the warehouse workers. This meant the sewing area was in a part of Patti's room and being used late into the night on some occasions. Patti never complained and usually sat nearby to watch her mother work minor miracles with a torn coat pocket or a dress too tight for the lady who bought it for the sale price rather than the size.

"Why do they buy those dresses too small in the first place?"

"Guess some ladies value price over honesty," Cassie answered as she let out another size ten seam for a size twelve body.

Now it was time to find another spot for all this activity and give Patti her privacy and space, even though the room was ever so tiny to start with. Cassie and John decided to add a small-glassed porch to the side of the house. This meant they would be very close to the next door neighbors who fought constantly.

"We'll just turn up the radio volume and drown them out," John said as he studied his plans.

Cassie would still have room to do her work, and on sunny days the family could cover the sewing table with a checkered cloth for a picnic lunch. The view from the porch, in addition to the neighbors' run down house and car on blocks in the overgrown yard, offered the outline of the Cleveland skyline. Smokestacks from the nearby factories belched out their refuse, and when mixed with the moisture in the air, made it impossible to see too far beyond, let alone breathe the intimidating air.

As she walked through the slushy grounds of the cemetery and made her way to the funeral home's car, Patti reflected on the past. It may not have been the most exciting, or prosperous, or successful, but it was in her eyes a happy life. "I will make a difference someday, I give this promise to myself."

CHAPTER TWO

THE NEXT TWO YEARS... found Patti living with a family from the church. A kind gentleman at the bank had taken over all of Patti's responsibilities, sold the house, and gave good accounting of the meager assets Cassie and John had left for her, their only living relative. The Meads, Helen and Glen, were members of the little Lutheran church where Patti and her family had attended services. They knew her parents as well as anyone could, which was not intimately, because Cassie and John did not get close to people. This was mostly due in part to their intense work schedules and lack of time for anything else but Patti's activities. The Meads had no children, but had a big house and hearts to match. They were glad to offer Patti her own room and asked only for a small amount of board, which she gladly paid from her babysitting money. The small amount of insurance from Cassie and John was added to her college savings and she eagerly watched it grow. Helen Mead delighted in having a "daughter" and never complained of the time she spent taking Patti to school plays, art exhibits, volleyball tryouts and then the games. John Mead, on the other hand, was glad Helen had someone else on whom to dote. Not that he did not like her attention, but he really preferred not having to answer her continual questions about insignificant

9

things… "Should we plant more roses this year or try some peonies? Do you think it will rain Saturday when we have the bazaar? Can you stop doing that crossword puzzle and fix the bathroom faucet that is leaking?"

In her senior year Patti made application to a small girls school in Batavia, Ohio. It was a liberal arts school, not too far from Cincinnati, where some of her friends would be at the University, and only a few hours from Cleveland. It was a happy day at the Mead house when the letter arrived from the scholarship committee, offering her a full four-year scholarship. The check they sent amply covered her expenses and she barely had to dip into the savings account.

"Mom and Dad Mead, I'm going to miss you, but keep watching the door, 'cause I'll pop back in often."

This sense of freedom was both baffling and exhilarating to Patti, for she was now on the brink of all she had been dreaming of for several years. "I'll work very hard and find that place for myself in the art world. Maybe the quiet, the lack of friends at home, the shock of losing Mom and Dad, have given me this need to pursue the solitary world of art, which can only be experienced by one's inner self." Never one to be the cheerleader type, the outgoing actress of the class, or the fanatical chemistry nut, Patti seemed to find her passion in reading about the great artists and in the tranquillity of viewing their marvelous works. She loved to share her ardor and intensity for this avocation, which she hoped, would become her vocation, but few of her acquaintances had the same enthusiasm for this beauty in life.

The thought of college brought challenges to her mind and body. Patti studied hard in high school and turned down every offer to date that came along. After her parents died she took new interest in her physical being, making some clothes that were more stylish than the ones she would just grab out of the closet without thought to color or match, and she had her hair cut into a short, attractive style. It was certainly a lot easier than dealing with those braids every day, and besides, they made her look so young.

Patti knew she had a goal to reach and would not accept any distractions... even if she longed to be with friends or experience the warmth of another person. The past couple of years had seen her slim little girl body develop into a tall, and very amply endowed figure. Not wanting to attract attention to this, Patti chose to cover her assets with loose jackets and baggy slacks. Good thing she could have this same style at college.

When not studying, babysitting or helping Mrs. Mead, Patti took part in the school art society and the honor society. As an invited member of the two societies, she found their meetings to be another stepping stone to her treasured goals in art. Most of the art society members were aspiring artists and the honor society members were there because they were superior students. Patti gained insight into the thoughts of the artist as she watched and listened to them present their works. Her contribution, for lack of a *product,* was enthusiasm and support.

Time drew near for graduation, and though it was sad to not have Mom and Dad there for sharing, Patti cheerfully went about her preparations for the big day in June. She accepted an invitation from Perry Kessler to the prom and then wondered why. Perry wasn't the best looking guy in the class, but at least he was presentable and she thought he had decent manners. She could have wound up with that klutzy football player who fell over Dad Mead's hassock when he came to pick her up for an art society meeting last fall.

Helen took great delight in shopping with Patti and treasured the time they shared. She also dreaded the day Patti would leave them in pursuit of her passion for art. After looking through all the racks of formals in most of the stores in town, Patti splurged on a crisp, new formal of white tissue taffeta. She also bought some white sandals and one of those little basket purses the girls were all carrying. Some of the girls added bouquets of flowers to the top, but Patti felt that was a bit much and not very classy at all. Bringing an end to a happy, but tiring day, Helen suggested they go to the Stouffer Inn for tea and pastry... one of Patti's favorite places, and definitely her favorite choice for sweets.

"Patti, I'm so grateful for being able to share your life. Your being with us has given Dad and me such pleasure and we hope you will always consider us family... next to your real mother and father." Tears in her eyes, she stirred her tea and watched Patti vigorously eat a large Napolean.

"Oh, Mom, you know you and Dad are special to me and I'll never really go away," she said, taking another bite of the cream filled pastry. "I'll just be back and forth more often than you'll probably like. I will have laundry privileges, won't I?" she asked with a mischievous smile coming from a face smeared with powdered sugar.

The prom was held in the school gym, and no matter how hard the committee tried, it still smelled like dirty sneakers and looked like a gym. If you closed your eyes you could think you heard the squeak of shoes and the tapping of a basketball as the team went dribbling down the court. The crepe paper streamers, the balloons and the foil stars could not transform this tired old building into the magical fairy tale place that all girls dream of for their final big dance in high school. At least the punch was tasty and the cookies had ample chocolate chips and nuts. Mom Mead headed up the food committee, so Patti had no doubt this part of the evening would be fine.

As midnight neared and the band played the familiar "Good Night Sweetheart", couples drifted off and headed for dark, quiet places where they might steal kisses and more. Some of the financially fit guys had rented fancy cars and had reservations at Rocky Creek Cafe for late dinner or breakfast. Several bribed older brothers to get rooms for them at the nearby Holiday Inn. Perry had made no mention of anything after the prom, so Patti assumed they would leave, drive to her house, she would offer a thank you and that would be the evening. Not so. With the rising hormones of a seventeen year old, Perry was sure Patti would at least want to take a drive near the lake. Or, he hoped she would.

They politely said good-bye to the prom chaperones, taking care to thank each one for the great music, food and decor (!), and walked slowly down the worn cement steps to the big steel doors that lead to the parking lot.

Nearing his dad's car, Perry said, "How about a drive by the lake and we can stop for a shake and fries?"

"Oh", she gulped, "I don't think so. I really have to get home soon, my folks are expecting me now."

With that he clumsily put his arms around her waist and pulled her to his chest. Struggling to free herself from this otherwise nice person, she dropped her bag and leaned down to pick it up. At that moment

14

Perry shoved her against the car and impaled his wet lips upon hers. He somehow opened the back door and, with decided determination, lifted her onto the back seat. Grappling to sit up, she was filled with surprise and disgust at his aggressive actions, but could not deny the strange feeling of some pleasure this was bringing. Once again she pushed to free herself and he fell out of the car like a beat little puppy.

"I'm sorry, Patti. But, you look so pretty tonight, we had such a good time and I thought you liked me." he said with a most defeated, but hopeful look.

"Oh, I did have a good time, Perry." she exclaimed with a nervous pitch to her voice, "but I just can't do that."

The ride home was unduly quiet. Since it was only a couple of miles from the school, they had no reason to try and make conversation when both of them were filled with questionable stirrings inside... he with unfulfilled longing, she with fright of addressing those stirrings.

Many times in the next few years she would ask herself, "Why do I have this inner unrest?" At times she struggled with feelings of desire but kept check on this, at least out in public. "Not now, time for that later," was always the answer from within.

College was all that she could now dream about and fall could not come any too soon. Once settled in Batavia, she quickly adjusted to

15

the different routine, made new friends, and fell into a pattern that allowed those dreams to materialize. She arranged and organized all of her classes and extra curricular activities to revolve around her goal of working in the field of art. As a music major would attend every concert possible, Patti scanned the newspapers for information on current art exhibits. If a friend were not available to go with her, Patti would go alone and savor the moments.

Getting a degree in art would enable her to find a job at a company like North and Associates, or some other large art dealership. They had business relationships with Sotheby's and Christie's in London and with other well known dealers of art in New York and Dublin. Dublin was a favorite city of the founder, William Lloyd North, whose mother was born there. Maureen Moriarity North, fled the Irish famine with her family for fortune in the United States. Working as a chambermaid in the old City Hotel in New York, she mysteriously met, fell in love with, and married William Vandermere North, son of a wealthy Madison Avenue art broker and a frequent guest at the hotel. Opportunities in the Ohio territory brought the North's to the shores of Lake Erie and the eventual start of North and Associates.

The North family of today, affluent residents of Shaker Heights and pillars of the social community in Cleveland, were known for their unmatched knowledge and appreciation of the fine arts, especially works from English artists…Constable, Gainsborough, Turner, and later artists like Lowdnes, Valette, and Shakelton, who all painted the English scene. William Lloyd North, after moving to Cleveland from New York, turned his art-collecting hobby into a business that sustained in fine measure his heirs. The large North building in downtown Cleveland, overshadowed now by the Ritz-Carlton Hotel and the Renaissance Cleveland, still found it's share of occasional sunrays coming down on Public Square and Superior Avenue. Customers of North and Associates came from all over the globe. Such would be the place where Patti wanted to work. So she persevered and endured to follow her dreams.

CHAPTER THREE

THE MEETING... was to be attended by a group of Patti's college friends who were coming together to view a recent art acquisition by the Vandermere Country Club for their newly redecorated boardroom. One night each month the group of ten very serious art students found a place to visit where they could enrich their hunger for both art and gastronomy. This time it was the old, but stately Vandermere Club. At 125 years old the club received a fresh look every ten years, needed or not. The renovation always included newly acquired works of art donated by members or their corporations. The club had been founded by William Lloyd North, and named for his grandfather, William Patrick Vandermere, of the New York Vandermeres.

The Vandermere Country Club was the social center for the Cleveland society leaders, and was located in Shaker Heights where the thousand elite members lived in estates with vast, wooded grounds, formal gardens, Olympic-sized swimming pools and substantial contingents of staff. Large though it was, the club was dwarfed by several of these *homes* of the successful residents, one in particular being the estate of William Lloyd North, Jr. and his wife, Marian.

Surrounded by buffers of tall cedar trees, the club grounds included a highly manicured golf course with thirty-six holes for play. Also for the member's use was a health club, three pools of various size and depth, a dozen tennis courts, four dining rooms serving divers cuisine prepared by world-renowned chefs, and several meeting rooms where more than a few multi-million dollar business deals had been sealed.

Earlier that evening Patti took care to dress, paying attention to her short blond hair, which she decided, could really use a trim. "Maybe tomorrow," she thought as she stared into the closet. The *little black dress with pearls* seemed appropriate for a classy place like the Vandermere and the old black coat would just have to do one more year. Laughing, she said out loud, "Guess the plain black pumps will make it one more season. If I can just find that black magic marker and cover up the scuff marks, no one will ever know," she smugly thought, proud that she was so resourceful, but careful not to bend the marker's tip. It was one she used for some serious drawings. "Someday I will not mend shoes and I will not check price tags before I try on a dress," she mused with determination.

Dad Mead had offered the use of his car for her trip to the Vandermere Club, but she thought it might look better if she arrived by taxi. The bus line stopped right in front of the club, but she would have to walk the long quarter mile of drive to the front door and probably would be joined by club staff. That would not look good, considering the occasion and the impression she wanted to make on her friends. Few of them knew where she lived or the circumstances surrounding her past, and she made no attempt to bring them into her confidence. "My past is my own, I shall let them be part of my future."

Alighting from the taxi at the front portico of the club, Patti was approached by a tall, extremely good-looking man with a very broad smile.

"Hi, are you waiting for the next bus?" he laughed as he asked. "Actually, I was waiting for my coach and six horses," came her quick retort.

"Sorry, you just looked like a maiden in distress and I would like to offer my help," he said as he checked her out from head to toe, noting with approval that he liked what he saw. She wore the perfect little black dress he had so often seen on his dates and her cute haircut framed a face that revealed a strange look of consternation.

"If you really want to help," she suggested, "you can direct me to the Boardroom."

"Well, gladly, Fair Lady, and whom do thee wish to meet there?" he said with a mocking tone to his voice.

"I'm meeting some friends to view the newly purchased *Scarborough Lights* by Atkinson Grimshaw," she answered, adding a smile.

"My, I am impressed. You know about Grimshaw?" he asked quizzically.

She hesitated for a moment and replied in a staccato manner,

"Well, yes, I was an art major and am very interested in the Victorian painters and I'm hoping to find a job with one of the art dealers here in town, now that I'm out of college."

The words came running out of her mouth so fast she knew it had to be someone else speaking. "Why do I feel so anxious right now?" She usually did not offer so much information, especially to strangers.

Not knowing how to respond to this fascinating and very pretty girl, he could only blurt out... "Why don't you come down to our offices and let me show you "my etchings". Oh, excuse me again, that's a tired old joke, but seriously, my family's in the art business and I'd be glad to see if we can help you."

With that, a group of six or seven laughing men came striding up to the front steps, slapped him on the shoulder and said,

"Let's go. The booze, the broads and the band are waiting for our charming company."

As he was being pulled hastily up the stairs by a hefty fellow in a gray silk Brooks Brothers suit, he reached into his pocket and handed her a card.

"My card, Fair Lady. Please call me, and have a good view of the Grimshaw. Good night." With that he disappeared beyond the heavy leaded glass door, his friends laughing louder than one would expect at such an elegant place like the Vandermere.

Turning the card over, Patti took a huge gulp of air and went into a most embarrassing coughing fit. "HE" was William Lloyd North, III, of "THE" William Lloyd Norths. "Oh, my word." she silently mouthed, as her surprise turned to hope. "Perhaps he just might be able to lead me to a job at his family's firm. It's sure worth a try."

Looking up she saw two of her friends arriving for the meeting. "Hi, Patti. Who was the hunk who had you so enraptured?", asked one of her inquisitive friends.

"Oh, just a member who was giving me directions to the Boardroom," she replied. And there was that feeling again.

They entered into the ornate foyer, with heavily carved wood stairwell and molded plaster-ceiling tiles, and proceeded to walk down a long, plushly carpeted hallway with gilt-framed paintings lining the walls. Passing two open French doors, Patti looked into the room and could see the opulence of decor in brocaded draperies, velvet covered settees and huge crystal chandeliers that reminded her of the Taverne in Richfield. Further down the hallway they stopped and were met by a man in tuxedo with a gold name tag reading "Rene."

"Good evening, ladies, I am to be your escort tonight for the viewing and then you have been invited as guests of Mr. and Mrs. William Lloyd North, Jr. to stay for dinner in the Regency Room."

Rene gave them a running description of the framed originals along their way and as they approached a back staircase curving to the next floor, he stopped. Looking at Patti he started to announce their entry to the library where the Grimshaw was displayed, when all of a sudden he uttered a muffled scream and grabbed her arm. She turned to help him and her eyes caught sight of why he had acted so peculiar. There under the stairwell, just five feet from the library door, was a girl who looked as if she were asleep. Rene collected his senses, bent down to the still form, and started to shake his head.

"The poor child is no longer of this world," he softly stated as his eyes circled the area obviously looking for something with which to cover her. She appeared to be in her late teens, was dressed in a uniform of the dining waitstaff and had a large amount of blood coming from her neck. Apparently her assailant was skilled with the knife... the one that was lying just beneath her right shoulder. He, or she, must have committed this grisly act and been scared away before disposing of the instrument of death.

Within minutes the area was filled with police and members of the club staff, including the general manager who stood silently weeping as he remembered the soft-spoken girl who joined his staff just last month. The girl was Amanda K. Bailey, an immigrant from England, who had taken this job to earn money for college. She was nineteen, frail of frame and had long, dark hair which she neatly wore in a bun when on duty. Amanda lived with her sister, brother-in-law and their little girl who had come to this country three years ago. She took well to the club ways, having worked in a small inn near Chester in England. There she not only waited tables, but helped clean the ten guest rooms, worked at reception, and assisted with answering correspondence from inquiring guests. With a dream to learn more about American standards of hospitality, she had hoped to attend one of the hotel schools and set her sights on Michigan State University in Lansing. The stop in Cleveland was temporary and she knew the experience at a fine club like Vandermere could only enhance her chances for acceptance. Now the dream was gone.

The police asked all of the evening's guests to please seat themselves in the ballroom, which had hastily been set with rows of folding chairs. One by one, they were each quizzed on what and whom they had seen that night.

"Did you speak to anyone other than your friends?"

"Do you know the victim?"

"How long were you in the ladies room, and did you see anything unusual in there?"

On and on they asked as the night grew late and Patti started to think of her busy day tomorrow and how the Meads must be worrying about her by now. A ruddy faced, Irish-looking policeman led her to a telephone and stood very close as she called home.

Finally, close to midnight and having been served no dinner except the trays of sandwiches that were passed around, they were told they could leave the premises. They were each given a card and asked to call the number listed if they could remember anything they felt would be important to the case.

Patti said goodnight to her friends and started down the steps when she realized she had not called the taxi company. She turned to go back in and bumped into...HIM.

"Still looking for the coach and six horses, Fair Lady?" he said with that same smirking smile in his voice and on his face.

"Actually, I forgot to call for a taxi and was going back in to make the call... that is, if they will let me use the telephone again. This has been a most disconcerting night." she expressed with both sadness and a bit of fear.

"If you would allow me, I'd be glad to drive you home. This has been an interesting night, that's for sure.", he offered as he waited for her reply.

Feeling a sense of relief and security, she answered, "Oh, that would be wonderful, but I'm sure it would be out of your way. I don't live near here."

"That's okay," he said, "I don't have an early meeting tomorrow and it would give me a chance to get to know you. Perhaps we can solve tonight's mystery and save the taxpayers some money." he joked. "Incidentally, I don't even know your name."

"Patti Hopkins." she quickly responded as he offered, "Well, I'm William North, and no, I don't go by Bill!"

"Hello, William North."

Walking in the cool early morning, on the way to William's car, Patti knew her life was taking a very drastic turn.

CHAPTER FOUR

THE TELEPHONE CALL... to William Lloyd North, III, was probably one of the hardest she would ever make. "What if I stumble on my words? What if I don't have the right answers to his questions? Worse still, what if he doesn't even remember asking me to call." All these negative thoughts went racing through her mind as she looked at the ivory instrument that would carry her voice to his. "Why am I so nervous about a job inquiry? He's just another man whose family just happens to own the leading art dealership in the country." But there was something about him that stayed in her mind from the time their eyes first met. Indeed, he was better looking than any man she had ever met, and he had such a pleasant smile. His clothes fit him to perfection and it was easy to see they were not off the rack. "He's probably never even stepped inside Higbee's," the local department store in Public Square, she thought. His dark, wavy hair was just above his collar and curled in a rebellious turn showing defiance of intent. The brown of his eyes gave a mischievous, yet warm appearance to an otherwise intelligent face. The surefooted gait he displayed when he approached her at the club gave a definite aura of confidence and self-assurance. "Why, why am I so uncomfortable with this encounter?" she again asked herself, as she contemplated the call.

Even the events of last night, "Oh, that poor girl," and the ride home, gave her cause for anxiety. She was glad it was so dark, making it hard to notice the very modest surroundings of the Mead house and the tacky yards of the neighbors. The murder at the club had made conversation difficult. Their minds running over and over what had happened caused question as to why anyone would want to kill a seemingly kind and innocent person.

William noticed that Patti was off in a dream somewhere and not really paying attention to his questions about her family.

"Sorry, I just can't stop thinking about that girl," she slowly said as she noticed they were getting close to her street.

She gave him a very brief bit of her family history and was quite relieved to see that she was almost home. He made no comment on the neighborhood or her story, but turned into the drive and shut off the engine of his new Mercedes coupe. Patti was so dazed and tired by now she didn't even notice the fine car. She was just glad to be home and wanted to run into the house and forget tonight's bizarre happening.

William stepped out and came over to open her door. As she reached up to accept his hand, he bent down and gently kissed her on the cheek.

"Fair Lady, this has been a memorable night despite the circumstances. You missed the dinner my folks had promised, so I offer a rain check and hope it'll be used soon."

"William, that is so nice of you. I apologize for being in such a fog the past couple of hours, but I've never had an experience like this. All I wanted to do was see the Grimshaw. Instead what we all saw was just grim. Do hope they'll find out who did this. That person could still be around your club. Oh, what a terrifying thought."

Sleep did not come easy that night. Patti's emotions were running rampant from fright to excitement to that old feeling again. William seemed to be two people… the playboy at the club and the gentle man who drove her home. Which one would she encounter when she called his office tomorrow?

The morning paper headlines told the story. *POSH VANDERMERE CLUB SCENE OF GRISLY MURDER.* The detectives from the Cleveland Police Department and the Shaker Heights force stated that the knife found near the body was a boning knife like those used in the club kitchen. They said the girl, who had been working there a short time, had only been dead for a matter of minutes when found by the manager who was leading a group viewing the club art collection. Further details of the murder would be revealed in the evening edition of the Plain Dealer.

As she entered the kitchen, Mom and Dad Mead looked up from their usual breakfast of eggs, bacon, toast and coffee. Dad spoke first.

"Patti, weren't you at the Vandermere last night?"

"Yes, Dad, I was there, and yes, I know all about that horrible incident," she replied as she wiped a tear from her eye. "That poor girl. It was awful, just awful."

Continuing on, she said, "We were just about to enter the library to see the painting when the manager grabbed my arm and there she was... dead, right in front of us. Oh, it was awful."

Mom Mead shook her head. "You must have all been terribly frightened. But, Patti, who brought you home? I heard a car door about one this morning, but was so tired I didn't get up to check. I thought you had gotten home hours before that."

Patti looked at her and said, "You probably will not believe this, but I met William North... the third... and he drove me home, would not let me call a taxi. He was very polite and we were both in such a state of shock that I hardly remember much about the ride. Really don't even remember telling him how to get here."

Helen Mead again shook her head. "You're right, I find that hard to believe."

"Well, it's true," she replied. "He and his friends came upon the scene right after we did and when the police arrived they made us all sit in the ballroom for questioning. William happened to sit next to me, but we didn't speak to each other. Guess we were all so shaken up and afraid to say anything. Then when they said we could go, I ran into him again at the front door as I was leaving the club. I'd forgotten to call for a taxi and afraid they wouldn't let me back in to use the phone. He offered to drive me home and by this time I was so grateful to just be going home that I would have taken a ride with the murderer himself. Well, not really."

Filling a mug with steamy coffee, she sat down to read the article. The description of the body and how it was found made chills run through her as she relived the night before. "And all I wanted to do was see the Grimshaw," she thought, almost with anger in her mind. But she also appreciated the fact that could very well have been her body on the floor. Who knows who the killer was or if he is still near the club. The article went on to say that the detectives were concentrating on staff who had access to the kitchen and the many tools of the chef's trade.

Patti quickly fell into her morning routine and barely caught the bus to her office. She had found a job at a small publishing company downtown on St. Clair and was assigned to cataloguing their backlog of unsolicited manuscripts. This certainly did not use her knowledge of the art world, but every so often a package would contain some sketches to go with a book and she enjoyed critiquing these for her own satisfaction. Only a short distance from the lake, Patti would occasionally walk to the shore and enjoy her lunch while watching the other lunch-break people who took advantage of a sunny day to escape dreary offices and driven bosses.

Today was one of those days when the sun was high in the sky, a gentle breeze was blowing and the air was clear. As she opened the plastic wrapping on a tuna salad sandwich, Patti was trying to plan in her mind what she would say to William when she made that special call. Almost choking on the first bite, she looked up to see him walking toward her on the sidewalk leading to the picnic area that she frequently made her lunch headquarters. "Do I look down and pretend I don't see him, or should I try to get his attention?" she asked herself as he got closer.

"Well, well, it's Fair Lady," he announced as he walked toward her table. "Do you lunch in the woods often awaiting your driver and coach?"

"Oh, William, hello. Good to see you," she answered. "This isn't too far from my office, so I come here to get away from the pandemonium of commerce."

"Well stated," he said.

"If you'd like to share a tuna sandwich, I have plenty. Joe's shop always makes them too generous anyway," she offered.

"Thanks, but I'm on my way to a business lunch at the Ritz and running a bit late as it is. Good to see you and hope you've gotten over last night's excitement. Don't forget to call me about that job," he called out as he turned and headed west to the Square.

"Thanks again for the ride home last night," she fairly shouted as he disappeared around a corner of holly bushes on the walk.

She watched as he waved and acknowledged. That feeling again.

CHAPTER FIVE

THE TELEPHONE CALL…was made and she did get the job as a junior appraiser for North and Associates. Fortunately she reported to one of the department managers and not to a North. That would have made life a bit difficult since she and William had started to date and for the past six months they were together a part of everyday. The courtship was way beyond the average person's perception. There were expensive gifts, numerous introductory parties, weekend trips to the North's various vacation homes, and always lots of people, people, people.

Patti did her best to avoid contact with William at work and that was not easy. The small office she shared with another junior appraiser was tucked back in the corner of the second floor. Customers and executives never had reason for straying into this dismal, dark area of an otherwise highly decorated business. But, appraisers had to be in all areas of the building, usually escorting customers to the appraisal rooms or to the offices designated for personal viewing of considered purchases. When the occasion did arise that they met, they kept their conversation on a very professional level. Once in a while the opportunity came about that William could not avoid. They would be alone and he would cautiously steal a kiss and a quick, but very tight hug.

From the very first date, when he took her to The Dining Room at the Ritz-Carlton, William's demeanor was always of a guarded manner. Patti could not figure out why he was so aloof at times and at others he was most affectionate. It did not seem possible that he was seeing anyone else since they were together almost every evening and most of the weekends. These *two Williams* confused her. Most of their dates were with his other friends, they were rarely alone. He seemed to have a very magnetic personality and people wanted to be with him. Conversations were mostly about the next sporting event, political races, new cars on the market, the state of the stock market, etc. Rarely did they talk about things that would interest the girls as well.

Patti tried her best to be a good sport because she was very fond of William, but the friends he had were so false. They were impressed with cars, finances and all the material things that money could buy. The girls especially were quite boring, most having limited vocabularies and bent on playing one-upsmanship on clothes and travel. Patti found it hard to join in, but held her own when they did manage to talk about the art world. Her knowledge surprised them and she guessed none of them knew she was not from *their side of the tracks.* William by now of course knew about her family and her present situation, but never brought it up in a derogatory or status manner. She appreciated his thoughtfulness, yet wondered how she would ever bridge this gap if they became serious. In the meantime, she enjoyed every day at work and looked forward to the ring of the doorbell and the sound of his voice. But, there were always so many people.

One evening, as dinner was being cleared from their table at the Vandermere, Patti excused herself to visit the ladies room. Following her was the latest date of William's best friend. The tall, buxom redhead was Paula Stratamondi, a former model who was now studying voice and hoped to leave soon for New York. Paula was the most talkative at the table that night and kept asking questions about the murder that happened there six months ago.

"William told us you were with the group that found the girl's body. Have they found the killer yet?" she asked as they both stood washing their hands at the green marble sinks.

Drying her hands on a white monogrammed towel, Patti answered, "I understand they're close to naming a suspect. Rumor has it that it's a local guy who was smitten with the girl and angry because she wouldn't go out with him," Patti grudgingly offered, thinking to herself, "Why can't she read the papers like the rest of us."

"The paper said she was an immigrant who had not been here long and was leaving soon to go to college in Michigan. Shame she had to die so far from her home and family," Patti added as she turned to leave the room.

"I met a guy recently who told me about his girlfriend and she sounded just like that girl. Wouldn't that be funny if it was her and he was the killer?" Paula laughed, and then taking a deep breath she added, "Oh, no, and to think I know who he is."

"You better call the police if you think you have some information. This could be serious evidence," Patti suggested as she wondered if this guy was one of the many guys who were always with their group. "Oh, probably someone she knows in the fashion world."

As they returned to the table the band was starting to play a Barry Manilow tune and she really wanted to dance. That was the only time she felt she was totally alone with William. Gliding around the highly polished oak floor, she felt lucky to be in the arms of someone so popular and powerful, and yet she felt that twinge of jealousy for having to share him so much. The music stopped and on the way back to their table William's arm was grasped and he spun around to find himself facing Paula.

"Hi, good lookin'," she said in a high-pitched voice. "I told your little date some info on the murder and she said I should go to the police. Figured since you're such a big shot around here you might think otherwise. I don't see anyone here that seems to be very concerned about it anymore, and it might even be one of you."

Caught by surprise and not knowing how to respond to this boisterous girl, William reacted in his smooth way, "That was very good advice and I suggest you accept it."

Patti appreciated his support, but was getting more uncomfortable by the minute being in this girl's presence. And tonight she was particularly tired of all the noise and all the people, people, people. Feeling a headache coming on she asked him if they could please leave. Remembering the customers coming in from Denver tomorrow only increased the tightening in her head. It was going to be a long and very intense day of gaining committal for some extremely expensive works by Charles Towne, the animal painter. She needed a good night's rest and not the persistent bantering of Paula.

Sliding onto the smooth leather seats of William's car, she leaned over and took his arm.

"Thank you for coming to my rescue from that person," she said as she tried to convey her feelings for his support.

"Oh, Paula, the put on", he answered, "Don't give it a second thought. She's a flamboyant gal who dotes on sensationalism. We'll all be glad when she goes to New York. Maybe they'll revive *Auntie Mame* just for her." Laughing, he started the car.

The cool night air gave Patti a shiver and she moved closer yet to William. As they drove through the gated entry of Vandermere, he took a turn to the right rather than the usual left.

"Know a new way home?" she asked.

"Just thought you might want to see the moon over the lake," he answered as they drove north toward Lake Erie.

In six months of dating, William had shown unusual reserve in his affections to Patti and with the slight amount of experience she had in this department, she knew it was not long before their relationship would have to change. Not knowing how that was to be, she could only hope that would be to intensify. There had been the gifts of flowers, jewelry, and even a painting from one of her favorite artists, Winslow Homer. This was not what she wanted to increase. She knew he was fond of her and always gave her long and arduous kisses, on occasion his hands had wandered to parts of her that responded in kind, but she never felt he was fully there for her. He had not yet asked her to come away with him to that place of ecstasy for lovers only. "Was this the night for change?"

The lights along the seashore illuminated the outlines of the buildings that had changed Cleveland's skyline in the past few years.

Here and there you could see couples strolling along that same walk where she used to take her lunch break. Slowing the car, William turned into a dark lane bordered by tall cedar trees. He pulled into a space narrowly wide enough for his car and turned off the engine.

Turning to her and putting his arms around her shoulders, he kissed her with a passion she had not known existed. It seemed ever so long before he withdrew his lips from hers, and placing his two strong hands gently on her smooth cheeks, he looked into her eyes and said,

"Patti, you are a most unusual girl, not like the ones with whom I've grown up. Not like the ones I dated in college, not like the ones you see at the club. I know you don't have the same past as mine and can't really change that, but we can have the same future… if you will marry me."

"I, I, I," she stammered as she fought back tears. "William, are you asking me or making a statement?"

"Fair Lady, I am asking you because for all the wrong reasons I have been trying not to fall in love with you and it didn't work. Patti, I know it won't be simple fitting into the life I have to lead, but you're bright and you can handle it. Besides, I have a feeling you love me, too. Just say, yes and let me get this darned box out of my hip pocket," he said as he lifted up his hip and struggled to get into his pocket.

Thinking that this was awfully quick and not exactly as romantic as she had dreamed, she was nonetheless thrilled to be asked.

There before her, catching the moon's rays on it's faceted surface, was the most enormous diamond ring she had ever seen. Surrounded by small sapphires in a square shaped setting, it both frightened and delighted Patti. William took the ring from its nesting place in the satin-lined box and slowly slipped it over her finger, moving closer to her as he did so. She threw her arms around his neck and kissed him with an ardor that surprised them both.

After several attempts to seal the moment with a more significant show of their love, it was William who *came up for air* and implied that they should leave before ruining the evening. "Ruin the evening?" she thought. "We're in love, engaged now and we can't be close?" Confused, she agreed, and he started the engine, pulled the car back into the drive and headed for her home.

The drive was unusually quiet considering the highlight of the night.

"Perhaps he's scared and just can't share that with me"

"Will she fit with the family and my friends?"

"Can I be the wife he needs and expects?"

"How much of my freedom am I going to lose with a wife?"

So much of this anxiety is normal for two newly engaged people, but these two in particular would have high bridges to cross.

Spring was a busy social time in Shaker Heights and Marian North's calendar was always full. Now William had interrupted her schedule to tell her that he had asked *that little girl from Woodland Heights* to be his wife. She found it hard to say her name. "Oh, she seemed like a bright girl and she was certainly pretty, but what could she bring to this marriage but herself. She had no family to speak of, lived in a sad part of town, had not been exposed to any social life as compared to William… and, she never seemed completely comfortable when she was with us." All these thoughts kept Marian concerned and very frustrated that she had to rearrange her social calendar to include showers, parties and then the wedding.

Frustrated or not, in her usual manner she tackled the job of selecting dates, places and the people who would be included in all of the festivities. Patti was told where and when she was to appear, what she should wear, and to whom she should show the most attention. The months of showers and parties leading up to the June wedding kept Patti on a treadmill of mixed emotions. On one hand she was so happy to be marrying William, but on the other she hated every minute of all this social life with it's facades of show. "These people are like masqueraders at a ball... you never really know who's behind the mask," she thought. William kept his distance throughout most of the planning stages and only appeared when his mother insisted she needed his input regarding his friends and their current dates or wives.

Patti had hoped to shop with Mother Mead for her wedding dress. So much for that hope. Marian North made reservations at the leading bridal shops in Shaker Heights, but was kind enough to invite Helen Mead to join them. Patti did insist however that the final decision on the dress, and the payment, would be totally hers. Knowing that she would not spend as much as Marian, Patti let her know that simplicity was her choice and it need not cost a fortune.

The selection of bridesmaids was still another *joint venture*. Patti had hoped to have just six of her friends from college, while Marian insisted she have the daughters of her best friends and this would certainly be fine with William because he grew up with all of them. In the end they wound up with fourteen bridesmaids and four flower girls, granddaughters of Marian's bridge club friends. Because Marian said they should stick with summer colors, the bridesmaids would be in pale pink and the flower girls in pale green. Marian chose to wear a sky blue gown from a new courtier collection and suggested Helen find something suitable in a beige.

Patti would liked to have had a small wedding in her little Lutheran church, but by now she knew that in *keeping with the program,* she would have to be married in the North's church, St. Luke's. It was old, dark and huge. "Good thing marriage ceremonies are short." She soon found out that was not the case with the North family weddings. The North family always had a full service including the Eucharist.

CHAPTER SIX

THE WEDDING... seemed to drag on for days, when in reality it would only be a few hours before they could leave Shaker Heights and be alone for three glorious weeks. Little did Patti know that those three weeks would also include calls to William's most important clients in New York, London and Dublin.

"So many appointments to keep, so many gifts to unwrap, all those thank you notes to write." Thinking she would never get it all done, Patti laid back in the blue chintz chaise lounge and closed her eyes. As she dozed off, a dream came to her where she was in a forest surrounded by tall cedar trees tightly keeping out the sunlight and offering no place of escape. Just as she was about to crawl through under a small tree, she awoke to find William leaning down to kiss her.

"Oh," she cried out as he jumped back. "I was having a terrible dream and you scared me, sorry."

"Just wanted to stop in and tell you that I am leaving for a couple of days to go fishing with the guys. It will clear my head for all the stuff we have ahead of us," he said as he sat down on the floor beside her.

"William, why do you have to leave now, when we have so much to do before the wedding? Your mother has so much scheduled for me I feel like the president with appointments from sunup to beyond. My dress is almost ready and I have two parties today, two tomorrow and, oh, my head hurts just thinking of all the smiling and thank-yous I'll be offering. It's so tiring." She tossed her head back on the lounge and then reached over to put her arms around his neck. "And why are you always with those guys? We never have any time alone and I have so many things I want to talk over with you." Near tears, the emotion and exhaustion of the past few weeks was catching up. Though she had resigned from the business... would not look good for the owner's daughter-in-law to be working... she had not had a day to herself. Marian North had every day planned, and most of it included *her* friends, not Patti's.

William tried to explain, but she tuned him out. Their entire courtship had been with friends. Even in a room full of people, Patti frequently felt quite alone. William was attentive, but he seemed to always have this need to be surrounded by people, people, and people. Maybe he was more clever than she realized. Being with others certainly prevented them from venturing into areas of activity that could compromise her values. But, she ached to be held more, to be told all the romantic things lovers speak of, to know the ecstasy of being one. With the exception of one weekend at the North cabin at Geneva-On-The-Lake, they were literally never alone.

It happened on a crisp, fall weekend when both of them found the unheard of *two free days*. Neither had any appointments or special social obligations, save the usual Saturday night at the Vandermere. William suggested they go to the cabin, and though she had not been there without the usual entourage of family and friends, she swallowed her fright and said, "Yes, yes, I want to go." In several months of dating, they had not passed the point of no return, not to say she was not disappointed in this and totally confused as to how William could control himself, but she accepted it as his way of loving her. And, she was not sure how to approach this part of their relationship, as she was certain he had had many romances prior to meeting her. She wondered if he knew she was a virgin and how, or when, would he change that?

Like everything else, their weekend was planned for them. Marian's housekeepers had prepared three boxes of food and supplies. They packed clean linens and included a new potpourri that Marian wanted placed in all of the bedrooms. Patti noticed as William was loading the car that someone, she presumed it was him, had also included several bottles of Dom Perignon champagne. Smiling to herself, she thought, "I think I'm in trouble and I can't wait."

The drive to Geneva-on-the-Lake took less than an hour. Passing some of Cleveland's seamier sides of life on their way out of town, Patti silently counted her blessings for her present and what was to lie ahead. "Oh, if only Mom and Dad could share these days with me", she thought, "I miss them so and they would have been so happy for me." It had been ten years since that terrible accident and never a day passed that she did not wonder how her life would be if they were still alive.

As they pulled into the long drive toward the lake, Patti caught a glimpse of a car leaving from the other side of the cabin. "Oh, no, are we going to be sharing the weekend with friends after all?" she asked herself.

"Wonder who that was?" William asked. The driver of the car waved as he pulled back onto the paved road. "Oh, I know. That was Jeff, the caretaker. He must have been here to open up and air the place out for us. Guess he got a new car, that's not his old clunker." She silently sighed with relief.

They gathered up all the boxes and their travel bags and went into the cabin. Built after World War II, the rooms were large with thick walls of stone. A huge fireplace was on the wall facing the lake and was banked by ceiling-to-floor windows offering a view of the imposing scenery. The kitchen was ample size and included all of the appliances necessary for a quick breakfast or a feast of freshly caught rockfish. Each of the four bedrooms had it's own bath, complete with jacuzzi. Furnishings in the cabin were surprisingly spartan, yet functional. Three down-stuffed sofas flanked the fireplace and a huge oak coffee table served all three. Marian had chosen navy, beige and red as her decorator colors for the cabin and kept true to this in all of the rooms, including the plaid of the draperies. A wide deck surrounded the entire cabin, and stairs in the back led down to a path to the lake. Both sides of the path were planted with seasonal flowers and this weekend the chrysanthemums were giving forth blooms of rust, gold and yellow.

At water's edge William's dad had built a boathouse and dock to store their three boats of various use. One boat was for skiing, one for fishing, and one for just plain cruising along the lake at sunset to watch the birds and ducks. Several varieties of ducks lived along the shore and the North's had placed birdhouses all over the property to encourage their habitation. Sitting in a rocker on the deck at sunset, with a glass of wine in hand, always rated big with both family and guests. The quiet, the view, and the peaceful surroundings made for a most pleasant experience.

Patti checked out the food they had brought and unwrapped two steaks in preparation for grilling. She washed some lettuce and put it in a bowl in the refrigerator, would add the tomatoes later. Picking two fat potatoes, she scrubbed them well and wrapped each one in foil for baking. All the while she was doing this she wondered what William was doing and where he had gone. Just as she set the oven to pre-heat, she turned and bumped into him. He smiled broadly, picked her up without warning, and kissed her with an intensity that sent chills through her and almost gave her cause for fright. As he set her back on her feet, he said, "Enough of this kitchen duty. I want you to come out on the deck. I have a surprise for you."

Through the screen door she could see some fishing paraphernalia on the picnic table.

"You, Mrs. North-to be, are going to learn to fish this weekend."

"I've never been fishing, William. I don't like to kill things."

"Fishing isn't killing things, silly. It's finding your food. And if it bothers you to have them die, you can throw yours back. Mine I'm going to keep and teach you how to clean and cook them."

This did not appeal to her and she was not looking forward to any part of it except the ride on the lake. "Oh well," she thought, "better get used to it. At least it's a way to be with him."

They sat on the deck drinking some Merlot wine the housekeepers had packed and made small talk about the lake, the cabin and the many times William had been here with all of his friends. She was extremely grateful they weren't here now. He started the charcoal in the grill and then sat in the kitchen watching as she finished the salad. She noticed that he kept looking at his watch and finally asked him, "Why do you keep checking the time? Are you expecting a call?"

"No, I just remembered that a couple of the guys and their dates were coming up to the lake, too, and thought they just might drop by."

"Oh, William, do I always have to share you with your friends?" she asked as she started to cry.

"Patti, they've been my friends for longer than I've known you and apparently you don't have the faintest idea how guys bond. You don't choose to have a lot of friends and I do. Get used to it, because it's not going to change." With that he went out to the deck, slamming the door behind him.

They had a very quiet dinner with hardly a word spoken. She cleaned up the kitchen and as she started down the hall to the bedroom he had chosen for her, she wondered if his friends were going to show up. It was about ten o'clock and if she had any ideas of an amorous evening, it seemed to go the way of the charcoal... burned out. She found her bag, and looking for her makeup kit, she also found the sheer, blue nightie she had bought just for this weekend. That was to have been the gown in which she would finally seal her love and commitment to him. Now she had doubts as to whether she even wanted to go on with this charade. "How could I be so blind?" she asked herself as she started to take off her sweater and slacks. "I know he must be seeing other girls, ones who will *comfort* him and take the pressure off our relationship. Am I just the sweet, innocent, look good at family and business functions, type? Have I been so stupid to not see that I'm part of a plan, a plot to let him continue his old life, but have the facade of the new one? Do I look that stupid that he thinks he can live around me and not with me?"

Just as she was about to step out of her bra and pants, she heard the door of her room open and in walked William with a bottle of champagne and two glasses. "Either get into something decent or out of everything altogether," he brusquely demanded as he poured the pale, bubbly liquid into the tall tulips. Unable to believe what he was saying, she stood there in amazement, shivering in the cool evening air.

It was evident that he had already sampled some of the champagne and it seemed he might have consumed more than she realized. She was now seeing the William who wore his shield of knighthood disguised as romantic and forceful. This approach certainly appealed to her emotions, but she had no idea how to control the feelings within that made her want to respond to his machonistic attitude. "Isn't this what I have been waiting for? Isn't this why I came up here in the first place?" questioning herself again.

Before she could take her choice of his options, he had grabbed her arm, threw her upon the bed and began to remove her bra and pants. In the midst of this outbreak he had had presence of mind to place the glasses on the nightstand. Taking one in each hand, he gave her one and said, "To this night, to the deflowering of my chosen bride, to the end of innocence, I drink to thee, Fair Lady." With that he downed the champagne and proceeded to refill his glass. Looking down at her naked and trembling body, he started to laugh and said, "What's wrong, didn't you think I was ever going to want to take you?" Sloshing through his words by now, he added, "It wasn't necessary to bother you and change you when there were always plenty of available bimbos around. But now that we're to be the next Mr. and Mrs. William North, I feel it is my duty to give you a small sampling of what life behind our bedroom doors will be."

Patti did not know whether to cry or laugh. She finally was where she had dreamed for so long and it didn't feel real. She was reaching for the blanket to cover herself when he fell upon her and began to kiss her with such force that she felt sure she tasted blood. The night was far different from the one she had pictured. And she, too, would now be different.

****

Christina's of the Gold Coast, on Lake Erie, was the leading bridal apparel shop in Cleveland, and though Patti really wanted to find her special gown at a less pretentious place, she gave in and went with Marian to Christina's. She did not expect to find what she had in mind, but was pleasantly surprised when one of the models came out in a dress exactly like she wanted. It was a long, form fitting, ivory satin gown with pearl embroidered high neck and cuffs, and had covered buttons from the back neckline to below the waist. With the exception of the pearls, it was perfectly plain and perfect for Patti. To flatter her face, Patti chose a headpiece shaped like a Jackie Kennedy pillbox. It was covered in pearls and from it fell a waist length veil of illusion. Since that night at the cabin, Patti's apprehension of this marriage was causing her to question her every choice. She felt trapped and unable to run from that which she had always wanted. Buying this beautiful gown represented her acquiescence to the situation and now she must *continue with the program.*

She awoke on her wedding day to the sound of Mom Mead starting breakfast in the big country kitchen. "I'll miss them and always be grateful for their love and genuine concern for me." Patti put on her old, frayed robe reminding herself to put it in the giveaway bag today, and started toward the shower. Poking her head into the kitchen. She blew a kiss to Helen.

"Morning, Mom. Sure smells good in there, but don't give me too much. I have those stupid butterflies in my stomach," she said as she thought about the next ten or twelve hours ahead.

The drive to the church took them over Van Aken Boulevard and to the corner of Warrensville Center Road. There on the corner stood the stately religious home for the North's of many generations, St. Luke's Episcopal Cathedral, diocesan center for Cleveland. Dad Mead refused politely the North's offer of a chauffeur driven limousine, choosing instead to rent a new Cadillac for their trip to the church. Once at the church, Helen and Patti went into the bride's dressing room and started to unpack her cosmetic bag. The bridesmaids started arriving and were directed to their special room and finally Marian came breezing in complaining about the traffic on Shaker Boulevard. "I cannot imagine where all those cars are going at eleven o'clock on a Saturday morning, really," she exclaimed. Her dress had been delivered with Patti's from Christina's and the bridal coordinator was there to help them get ready. Since Marian had enlarged the guest list to five hundred, Patti could only think all of those cars were coming here to the wedding.

The priest, Father Charles Downing Satterfield, flatly gave forth with the marriage service and weakly smiled as he asked Patti and William to speak their vows. Followed by the Eucharist, which was taken by most of the wedding guests, the organist loudly played the traditional Episcopalian recessional music, John Stanley's *Trumpet Voluntary*. As they passed the flower-bedecked pews filled with smiling faces, William held Patti's arm tightly, looked deeply into her eyes and seemed to be sincerely there with her alone. Or was this just a wishful illusion?

It seemed to Patti that there were thousands of cars following them to the Vandermere for the reception, when actually there were nearly three hundred. The club staff had given this wedding event their very best efforts, full well expecting handsome gratuities from Mr. North. The main ballroom was decorated in Marian's pastel choices. Pink cloths covered the tables and very tall bouquets of summer flowers with miniature musical instruments were on each table. The buffet tables were laden with every imaginable luncheon delicacy and the six bars offered choices of only the finest labels.

Patti excused herself to the ladies room as they arrived and when she came out she was greeted by a long line of William's friends, all holding out a glass of champagne and shouting to her, "Welcome to this part of the world, Mrs. North." Did she imagine they were insinuating that she was not part of it until now?

The ten-piece orchestra was playing "Embraceable You", an old song that Patti and William danced to on one of their first dates. *"I love all the many things about you... want my arms about you..."* William, who was talking with his friends, came across the polished floor, took her arm and led her on to the dance floor. He held her very tightly as they danced and spoke all those things that a bride wants to hear on her wedding day. "If only this would stay, and not the phony order of most days," she wished.

People, people, people... three hours at the reception and she was so tired of meeting, thanking and smiling. Besides, her satin shoes had gone beyond the pinch stage to the torture vise stage. Finally she got the message from the bridal coordinator that it was time to change into her going away outfit. "Going away. Away from people, people, people."

CHAPTER SEVEN

THE SOUND OF SIRENS... filled the air and were heard over the music of the dance band. Patti was changing out of her wedding gown when through the door came Marian, white as a ghost.

"The police are here and they want to question William and his friends about that girl's murder late last year. Oh, dear, not on his wedding day." She fell into a nearby chair and started to cry.

"Good grief," screamed Patti, "Why would they wait until today of all days? And, it's MY wedding day, too," responding assertively.

The officers discreetly approached William and asked him to follow them to the Boardroom... that same room where they had gone to see the Grimshaw painting. As they entered the room, William saw the manager, Rene, sitting in a chair at the back, looking quite frightened. The officers motioned to William to take a seat, followed by five of his groomsmen who came in and were seated.

All of their questions seemed routine and senseless, given the fact that it had been so long since this happened and with their full knowledge that each of them had accounted for their whereabouts that fateful night. Still, they had to endure this unpleasant episode in an otherwise very happy day. Rene did not utter a word, but kept his steely black eyes focused on William.

Almost as abruptly as they appeared, the officers began to leave the room, seemingly satisfied with the information they had received.

"Now that this day has been ruined," William remarked, "Guess I'll collect my bride and try to make it to the airport before we miss our flight to New York." He stormed out of the room and hastily walked down the hall to the bride's dressing room, almost knocking over a waiter who was delivering still another tray of champagne to the guests. As he started to knock, the door opened and his mother stood there staring at him.

"What did you tell them?" she asked with a show of terror in her eyes.

"Why, the truth, of course. I didn't see anyone suspicious that night, certainly no strangers. I was here with the guys and our dates. Actually, Mother, I don't think there were many non-members here that night anyway, except the girls who were here to see that painting. Looked to me like whoever killed that girl would have had to be pretty skilled with the blade and I don't believe Patti or her friends had that talent."

Looking behind his mother, William could see that Patti had changed into a pale blue suit and was anxiously trying to leave the room.

"Let's go, Fair Lady," he called out, reaching for her hand, "We have a plane to catch and a life to start." They brushed past Marian, William pausing to kiss her on the cheek and then they ran down the hall toward the front door and the waiting limousine. The wedding party and guests all began throwing rose petals in a halo of cheer. Patti looked for the Meads, but could not find them in the crowd. Perhaps they were still dancing, but she doubted they would miss her departure.

Just as the limo driver opened the door of the sleek black car, Patti heard Mom Mead call out, "Happy life, Patti. You deserve it." She waved and blew a kiss.

The drive to the airport was swift due to the delay with the police. Patti asked William what had happened. His response was obviously a conversation he wanted to discard.

"They kept wanting to know where we were, who we saw, all that kind of stuff. We had already told them this several times the night of the murder and later when some detectives visited our offices. I don't know why they keep on us like this. None of us, to my knowledge were involved in this mess. Anyway, I have to call them every few days to stay in touch. Can you imagine, here we are going on our honeymoon, and I have to report to the police. I feel like a criminal and my only crime is being a member of Vandermere and just happening to be there that night." Deep in his mind though, he kept visualizing Rene and his glare, noting that there was something strange about his behavior and lack of communication with anyone in the room. He had always been a very friendly and gregarious man. Maybe he knows who killed the girl.

As it had been for years, Cleveland Hopkins Airport was undergoing another sizable renovation, which included tearing up part of the entrance and rerouting traffic for departures. The limo driver, unfamiliar with the changes, had to ask for directions from a policeman and about now William was getting terribly impatient and concerned that they would miss their flight to LaGuardia. Finally able to reach the correct departure area, Patti and William hailed a skycap and in a few minutes their luggage was loaded and they were on their way to the Delta gate. At the gate they were greeted by a Delta Redcoat Agent and quickly escorted to the plane, which had already started boarding. Seated in first class, the flight attendant welcomed them and presented Patti with a bouquet of red roses. She then proceeded to pour glasses of champagne.

"Funny thing, Patti, I can't forget the look of Rene's eyes during the last questioning session. I think he either knows who did it, or he's the murderer. It just doesn't add up. He knew her. In fact, he was one of her managers. He found the body, and he sits mute. There's got to be a reason for his strange behavior. His duties require him to be very visible and know what's going on in the club at all times. Maybe he's covering for someone else. You'd think the detectives would have something concrete by now," William mumbled as he raised his glass to Patti.

"William," she said, taking a deep breath, "I am so happy, and so sorry that your part of our special day was spoiled by that murder thing. Please try to get it out of your mind and just think about us."

Raising his glass, he said, "Okay, Fair Lady. I'm now all yours. At least until we get to New York. I meant to tell you that I have some meetings scheduled there with the Christie's people. They have some new estate acquisitions I need to look at and this seemed the logical time to do that. Hope you don't mind. You can keep busy shopping on Fifth Avenue, or getting a facial at Elizabeth Arden's."

"Are you insinuating that my face needs help?" she jokingly asked.

"Of course not, your face suits me just fine. It's just that I really need to do this and I don't like to shop. You do understand, don't you?"

The plane rolled down the runway and they gently took off to the east and what she hoped would be more than just a romantic honeymoon. She wanted to really get to know William and his deepest thoughts, his plans for their future and his reasons for the need to constantly be surrounded by friends. In the time they had been dating, there never seemed to be the perfect moment for talking about these things. Now she would be alone with him in strange cities. Well, they were certainly strange to her, but he had been in them often, as a child and as an adult. Guess that means he has friends there.

The flight, short and smooth, hardly gave them time to sit back and relax, when the announcement of their approach to LaGuardia came over the speakers. Another long limousine was waiting to take them over the bridge and into Manhattan. Down along the river and turning on to Sixty-second Street, the driver dodged traffic and eventually pulled up in front of the Plaza Hotel. Patti looked up at the lighted facade of this historic building and was filled with anticipation. She smiled at the passing horse drawn carriages, taking tourists for their first glimpses of the big city. Since the hotel was across from Central Park where the carriages parked, Patti hoped they, too, would take a ride. She wanted to see the buildings that shaded the light from the streets with their height, the theatre marquees announcing the latest stars, the Fifth Avenue shops with all of their finery, the delicatessens with windows of sausages and olives, the linen shops always going out of business and even the sad street people who gave this city it's flavor and character.

The front desk clerk barely raised his eyes to them as they approached the counter. William cleared his throat and slapped his platinum card on the cold marble as the clerk looked up.

"Oh, Mr. and Mrs. North. We've been expecting you. It's not necessary for you to check in here. The concierge will take you to your suite. Do hope you will find everything in order." With that he went back to whatever was taking his attention on the lower counter.

They followed the concierge to an elevator with antique brass doors and bronzed mirrored walls. Hoping the mechanism was not as antique, Patti squeezed William's hand as the elevator stopped at the tenth floor and their private suite. The ivory doors, heavy with molding, were open and revealed a sitting room, dining room and bedroom area, all decorated in shades of yellow, cream, gold and white. The furniture was heavy French and the window dressings were brocade with ornate design and braided trim. On the dining room table was a huge bouquet of summer flowers, obviously ordered by Marian because they were exactly like the ones at their reception. A bowl of caviar and toast points was adjacent to champagne chilling in a cut crystal container, while at the other end of the table there was a basket of exotic fruits dressed with breads of various origin. To Patti this looked like a table ready for guests at one of the North parties, which usually numbered at least one hundred guests.

William discreetly gave the concierge and bellman a generous tip and came in to the dining room where he poured champagne into the waiting Tiffany glasses. Patti had gone into the bedroom to take off her jacket and take a quick glance of herself in the mirror.

"Can't believe the dream has arrived, but here it is," she thought.

"Hey, Fair Lady. You gonna stay in there or come out here and enjoy the champagne with your husband?"

Husband. That sounded so strange to her, and yet the day had given them new definition. Suddenly memories of that night in the cabin at the lake ran through her mind. She tried to squelch the thoughts and slowly walked back into the dining room to join William.

"Thought you might have been in there getting into something more comfortable," he said with a smirk on his face.

"Oh, I'm quite comfortable," she nervously answered as she accepted the glass from him.

"To my Fair Lady. May I make her happy and may she always understand I am what I am," he said as he bowed slightly to her before joining her glass with his.

She took a sip, and placing her glass on the polished mahogany table, stepped close to him. He moved closer to her and they were in each other's arms, kissing with a passion and expectation of things to come.

Unpacking her Vuitton luggage, a shower gift from Marian's bridge club friends, Patti took out her gown and robe, a beautiful creation from Christina's. She had seen it the day she went in for her second fitting of the wedding gown. The robe, of ivory silk charmeuse was detailed with lace and pearls, the matching gown had softly gathered straps, and not the thin *spaghetti* straps usually found on this type garment. Satin slippers completed the outfit which Patti felt was a waste of money because it would not be in use for very long. She brushed her teeth and peeked around the bathroom door to see if William was in the bedroom. There was a small lamp next to the bed and it obviously had a very low wattage bulb, because she could hardly see anything in the room, let alone William.

As she cautiously measured her steps into the darkened room, she heard William speaking to someone in the next room. Much to her relief, he was only on the telephone, but seemed to be engaged in a very heated discussion with someone. After a few minutes he put down the receiver and walked toward the bedroom and Patti.

"Who was that?" she asked, watching him kick off his shoes as he started to unbutton his shirt.

"Oh, just one of the guys. They wanted to surprise us and come up for a couple of days. I knew how happy that would make you, so I told them to forget it," he said very sarcastically.

"William, can't we even have our honeymoon to ourselves? I know you love your friends, but our lives are different now and we have to think of each other first," she said as she followed him to the bathroom door.

He just glared at her like that night in the cabin. Slamming the door, then turning on the shower, William was fighting to control his emotions. He took a quick shower, wrapped a towel around his tight, lean body and came out into the bedroom. Patti had turned off the little light and as he stepped over the threshold he went flying on to the floor, at the same time shouting a few choice expletives. He had tripped over her silk slip, which had fallen off the door hook and on to the bedroom floor as he opened the door.

"William," she screamed, "Are you alright?"

"Yeah, sure. I think I just broke every bone in my lower body, but I'll be fine. Move over, and from now on, keep your clothes off the back of the door." Was this the gentle man she met last year, who impressed people with his manners and his smile?

After a few minutes of silence, he rolled close to her, and finding that she was still in a mass of clothes, started to improve the situation.

Not knowing whether to forget the recent outburst, or to address it, she let her quivering body rule her mind. Searching for the best in innocent seduction that she could muster, Patti responded to William's love with an eagerness that challenged them both. He was not aware, due to his choice, that she was capable of such ardent lovemaking and began to wonder how and when this educational process entered her life. And, who were her teachers. These questions quickly passed as they both transposed thoughts of their expectations into fulfillment of their love.

The following morning, after a sumptuous breakfast in the Palm Court, William told Patti that he had tickets for that evening's performance of *Cats* and the next night they would be seeing *Chorus Line.* He also informed her that he had a late morning meeting and another in the afternoon. Would she mind very much shopping and he would join her later for dinner before the theatre?

Patti walked down the stone steps of the Plaza, turned left onto Central Park South, looked longingly at the carriages and then proceeded to Broadway. She had always wanted to walk all the way from the Park to the theatre district, and although some blocks were safer than others, she continued on her way. Passing shops selling everything from cameras to china dogs, she looked ahead and saw the big clock at Times Square. Making a turn onto 46th street, she stopped at a *Dean & Delucas* for coffee and a parmier. It was so lonely, even with all those people rushing to wherever they were all going. Further down Broadway she turned left on 38th street, and seeing a ribbon and trimming shop went in. The walls were covered with every possible type of ribbon, braid, embroidered trims, and buttons. She bought several yards of ribbon for Mom Mead who liked to make pillows. Feeling proud that she had spent some of the money William had given her, she made her way to Fifth Avenue and Lord & Taylor's on the corner. Patti browsed through the designer clothes, saw none that interested her, and took an escalator to the childrens' floor. "Why would I want to look at childrens' things," she questioned herself. "William and I have barely mentioned having a family. Oh well, it's different and I'm bored."

Fifth Avenue, with all of its glitzy shops, was crowded with shoppers. Patti especially enjoyed looking in the bookstores, of which there were many. A large part of one block further north was being developed and it was said that a wealthy young man was going to name the tower after himself. It was to be shiny gold on the outside, like a Christmas package. "That will be a sight to see," she thought as she crossed over to a church on the other side of the street. Looking inside, she could see beautiful stained glass windows illuminated from behind and the sound of soft organ music coming from the sanctuary. She stepped inside, slipped into the end of one of the pews and closed her eyes. "Dear God, please bless our marriage. I am so confused and afraid of this person to whom I am now joined. Show me the way, Lord."

Almost back to the Plaza, she went into Bergdorf Goodman and found a fine pair of leather gloves for William. Even though the weather outside was summer warm, she knew fall would bring cold days to Cleveland and seemed to remember his gloves always looked worn. This, too, was strange to her, since he was usually impeccably groomed. On the way out she passed a counter displaying small gold angels. Finding one that she liked, she gave the clerk a crisp hundred-dollar bill, accepted the small amount of change and pinned the angel to the collar of her suit. "Now, I have bought my first piece of jewelry as Mrs. William North, III. Won't Marian be pleased," as if she had to do this.

The next few days were the same as the first. She shopped, he met. Evenings they went to one of New York's best restaurants and then the theatre, which she adored. Later they adored each other.

At the end of the week they flew on Aer Lingus to Dublin. Patti was very excited to be visiting the country where William's great grandmother had been born. Prior to the wedding, she read several books on Ireland and tried to show William her interest in this part of his life. He, on the other hand, chose to leave her to her reading, while he researched artist's works that were available for the business.

They had rooms at the new luxury hotel, The Westbury on Grafton Street. In the premier business and shopping district, it was only a short distance from the National Gallery and Trinity College where William would do his research. About six blocks from the River Liffey, Patti could easily walk there in the afternoon while she waited for him to return to the hotel. Dublin was not as exciting as New York, of course, but the people there were very genuine in their communication with others. She loved watching the pink-cheeked children with curly ringlets of varying shades of red. They all laughed so much. "Oh, how I want to laugh more," she longingly thought.

One afternoon, as she sat on a park bench in St. Stephen's Green, she noticed a priest coming down the stone path toward her. Approaching her, he tipped his head and said, "Aye, good day, miss. Are you enjoying watching those wee babes at play? Aren't they a precious sight for the eyes?"

Without hesitation, she replied, "Oh yes, they are all so pretty, too. Would you care to sit and watch, Father?" she asked.

"Thank you, dear lady, but I have to get to Trinity College for a meeting. I'm not from here, you see, only here on church business and then I go back to my parish in England."

71

"We're going to England next week. Where is your church?" she asked this intriguing young man.

"Oh, you've probably never heard of it, it's just a small village in Suffolk, north of London, called Kersey. But if you and your husband get that way, please do come to see us," he invited as he noticed her large wedding ring set. "Enjoy the wee ones and have a safe journey," he offered as he continued down the path.

As he left she felt an indescribable feeling of love flow through her being. It was not a feeling of lust, but rather one of peace and courage. Thinking she must be tired, she added this encounter to others in her life where she had briefly met people who made a difference. Sitting straight up she realized that the village of Kersey was one she had heard about from a college friend. Interesting!

On Friday they flew to London's Gatwick airport. Their limousine had been delayed by one of the city's notorious traffic jams, so they decided to be *common tourists*, take the train into Victoria Station and then a taxi to their hotel. Except for the hassle with their luggage, they both rather enjoyed this change in plans and had a good time watching people and making up stories about who they were. The taxi drive to the Dorchester Hotel was quick, and although Patti would liked to have stayed at a less pretentious place, the Dorchester was most elegant. Their room was small by American standards, as were all English hotels, but the service was beyond reproach. They seemed to bump into staff at every turn. Overlooking Hyde Park, the hotel appealed to international guests of great renown.

London turned out to be just like New York and Dublin. Her days were her own and she was by now beginning to like this arrangement. The evenings were her reward for this endurance.

One misty London morning she took the tube to Knightsbridge Station, walked through *Harrods* and then strolled down Cromwell Road to the *Victoria and Albert Museum*. On the way she passed a small travel agency, *Cadogan Travel,* and stopped in to ask directions to Kersey, just in case they could go there one day. At the *V&A,* as they call it, she slowly visited many rooms of antique dress, musical instruments, weapons of war, Oriental art, and furniture of the past. Yet, in the hours she was there, it was impossible to see it all. She told herself she would come back and hopefully William would want to come with her.

William's meetings at *Christie's* and *Sotheby's* were successful and he came back to Cleveland with a briefcase full of potential purchase orders. Patti's self-escorted tours had given her a new insight into other people and cultures. She loved the warmth of the Irish, the confidence of the English. She loved Irish Stew and English scones. Together, yet apart, they both enjoyed the honeymoon.

CHAPTER EIGHT

THE FIRST YEAR... filling her time as expected of all young brides in the North family, she dutifully hosted bridge luncheons (and abhorred the game), was a member of the hospital auxiliary, played golf once a week with the nine-hole group, lunched with all the proper young matrons in the city, and skillfully planned and implemented dinner parties for William and his father's best clients. She attended all the birthday and anniversary celebrations for the North's, and accompanied William on business trips to exotic resorts and foreign countries.

To the average person this kind of lifestyle would all seem very exciting and fulfilling. To Patti it was a waste of time, talent, and the energy she could be spending on her marriage. With the exception of her hospital work, it was all such a false existence. Everyone seemed to smile from behind clenched teeth, wishing they, too, were somewhere else, or smiling broadly to impress the boss and his wife. Patti's manners were impeccable, her speech eloquent as any studied actress, and her sense of style was comparable to that of Jackie Kennedy. She knew how and when to say the right thing, who to compliment, and exactly when to come across as shy and retiring. Her transformation from a simple girl in Woodland Heights to a welcome young matron in Shaker Heights was almost complete. To all outward observations, she was a happy and contented lady, who possessed all the material things necessary to make her the consummate bride of one of the city's most successful young businessmen. While inside this shell there dwelled a most confused and frustrated soul. She constantly wrestled with her emotions, wondering why she could not find total contentment in something. There was always a full calendar of social engagements waiting and that took up her time with shopping, planning wardrobe, visits to the hair salon and correspondence related to these events. Evenings were usually crowded with dinner parties in clients' homes or in their own, boring cocktail functions where she was expected to smile a lot and make small talk, or charity events where she was more than not on one of the committees. How she wished for a whole month, or even a week, when she and William could go away, alone, and spend some quiet time. They were always surrounded by people, people, and people.

****

One Tuesday morning while delivering mail as part of her hospital work, she noticed an envelope with Perry Kessler's name on the return address. Not having thought of him in a long time, she was curious to see to whom this mail was going. It was addressed to Miss Nancy Cole in the pediatric ward. She put the envelope in her pocket, finished delivering mail on the surgical floor and then took the elevator to the third floor pediatric area.

"Good morning, Miss Forrest." Greeting the charge nurse as she made her way down the hall, Patti stopped at room 302. Gently knocking, she heard a small voice call, "Come in."

"Hi, I'll bet you're Nancy Cole," Patti said as she walked over to the bed. There laid a beautiful little girl of about six with long blond hair and big blue eyes.

"Yes, I'm Nancy," she answered as she struggled to sit up, "Who are you?"

"My name is Patti North and I'm a volunteer. I do lots of things like deliver mail to pretty little girls like you."

"You have mail for me?"

"Yes, and it's from a man I used to know in high school, Perry Kessler. How do you know him?"

The child turned her head toward the window and started to cry. Not wanting to frighten her, Patti slowly approached the side of the bed and softly said, "I didn't mean to upset you. You don't have to tell me. It's alright."

"He was a friend of my auntie's and he hurt her. I'm not supposed to tell," she cried. "Please don't let him know I told you. I don't want him to hurt me, too. I miss her. She came to visit us from England and was going to teach me how to make scones."

"Oh dear," Patti said, "Does anyone else know he hurt your aunt?"

"No, but he came by our house after she died and gave me a doll and some books. And he told me he was sorry. I was afraid of him."

Not wanting to further upset the child, Patti smoothed the covers and put her hand out to pat the trembling child. At that moment the door opened and a lady entered carrying a bouquet of daisies.

"Mommy, mommy, I'm so glad you are here," Nancy said as she wiped her tears with the blanket.

"Why are you crying?"

"Oh, I just got a shot and this nice lady came in to tell me it will make me feel better," she said, trying not to show her fear of the recent conversation.

"I'll be going now. Hope you feel better, Nancy." She slipped the envelope back into her pocket and hoped the mother did not see her do this.

The next morning Patti thought about the little girl and her fright at the mention of Perry's name. She said her aunt had just come from England and had died. This was beginning to be a bit too coincidental. Not knowing whether to call William and tell him her concern, or whether to call the police, she got into her car and started driving to the old neighborhood. She passed the school and thought of that prom night and Perry's crude efforts at being romantic. It made her shudder as she remembered the look in his eyes as she pushed him away. "Could this same boy be the person who murdered the girl at Vandermere, or am I projecting?" She had read horror stories of men who killed for being rejected. "Didn't the detectives say the girl was killed by someone whom she had declined to see? Surely this is just a coincidence, but why was that little girl so frightened, and why would she tell me, a stranger, about this event?"

Patti pulled into the familiar driveway at the Meads and was glad to see a light on in the kitchen. That meant Mom Mead was home from work and probably about to start lunch. She knocked, and fairly leaped into Helen's arms when she opened the door.

"Oh, Mom, I'm so glad to see you. I have something to discuss with you and it's very frightening," she blurted out as she took a chair from the round oak table. Sitting down, she started to tell Helen the details of yesterday's visit with little Nancy Cole.

"Mom, do you think there is any way Perry could be the one who murdered that girl? I thought about the dates and it seems to fit. But I haven't heard anyone mention his name for a long time."

"Patti, it seems to me that someone told me he moved away to New York several months ago. He was a strange boy, Patti. I didn't want to ever tell you this, but he came by here a few days after your wedding announcement was in the paper and told me you were not the girl everyone thought. He told me that he and other boys had *had their way with you* and he was going to let your new friends know. Dad and I gave him five hundred dollars and told him to never show up here again and if we heard that he bothered you we would go to the police. It was soon after that we heard he left town." She was crying and came over to sit beside Patti.

"Oh, Mom, I am so sorry. But you have to know that I never was that kind of girl. I couldn't have done that to you or my parents. He tried to get fresh with me on prom night and I had to fight him off. After that night he never spoke to me. Guess I don't blame him, when all the other girls were playing the game."

Helen hugged her and got up to put on the tea kettle. "Honey, I believe you now and never did doubt you. He was an evil boy and scared the living daylights out of me. Good thing Dad was here, or I might have done something we would all regret."

Pondering all this, Patti stirred her tea and as she put her cup down, she looked at Helen with anger and fear in her eyes. "What do I do now. I really don't want to get mixed up in this, but if I can help solve the case, it would help that little girl and relieve her fears. I can just see Marian's face when she hears about all this. Ha, I'll probably be booted out of the family."

"Follow your own feelings, Patti."

She kissed Helen, asked her to give Glen a big hug, and got back into her car. All the way back to Shaker Heights she kept wondering if this was a dream, a coincidence, or the real thing. "Guess I have no choice, I must go to the police. But first I'll tell William and hope he'll understand. When she got home she found the Kessler number in the telephone book. Gingerly picking up the telephone, she dialed and waited for an answer.

"Hello," said the lady on the other end of the line.

Taking a deep breath, Patti said, "May I speak to Mr. Perry Kessler, please?"

"I'm sorry, he no longer lives here. Who's calling?"

She was too frightened to answer and immediately hung up.

"Well, at least he isn't at his parent's home," she thought.

The next few weeks were filled with meetings with the detectives, newsmen and television reporters. Patti had given the police the envelope and information that lead them to the murderer. It was Perry. They found him living in an apartment of putrid squalor on the lower east side of Manhattan. It was not necessary that he live in such filth, as he was bartending in a hotel lounge at night and working in a garment warehouse during the day. The police found several thousand dollars stashed in a bag in his closet and surmised that he was saving to leave the country. A recent passport was in a nylon sports bag and brochures on England were in a dresser drawer. Patti wondered if in his warped mind he intended to find her family and make amends. "He did try to be kind to the girl's niece, didn't he?"

William and his family were more patient than Patti had hoped for, but Marian kept her distance and never brought up the subject of *that nasty situation.* William did however start to spend more time, if that was possible, with his friends. He had breakfast meetings, luncheons, dinner meetings, conferences, tennis matches, golf games, and other places to go where it was obvious he did not want her in attendance with the possibility of questions about the murder. It was bad enough that they still had to keep up appearances at several social functions during the month. It was interesting to note that none of her friends seemed to make much mention of her involvement, and when they did it was only to commend her for coming out with the information. It seemed Patti could not win with the family.

As the time drew near to the holidays, William told her to cut back on accepting invitations. He said he had a heavy business travel schedule and would choose the few he wanted to attend. This first year of their marriage had not been at all what she had dreamed. Sure there was the big house, the new cars, the fine clothes, the expensive jewelry, all those *things*. But they never had time to be alone and close. She longed for private time and just about the time she thought they had worked this out, the Perry Kessler situation arose.

Often Patti let her thoughts lead into dreams of a family... her own family... one where she and William would have children and he would pay attention to her and them. But with each passing month she felt the disappointment of that dream and was beginning to feel that perhaps it was not her lot in life to be a mother. Not wanting to dwell on this, she busied herself with holiday chores. Shopping with an unlimited expense account was not fun, it was overwhelming, because she felt expected to come forth with original gifts for the entire family. So she tried a themed giving attempt and bought something for everyone in blue. If it was a shirt, it was blue. If it was a book, the jacket was blue. And of course, the wrappings were blue paper and blue bows. When she tried to decorate the tree with all blue lights, ornaments and tinsel, William stepped in and gave a firm, "No way!" Well, at least it was original and not that same overdone, heavy on tradition, look that Marian insisted on each year. "Della Robbia probably got its start with Marian," Patti laughed. Patti tried so hard to be herself, but always wound up pleasing the family and all of the friends... all of those people who were constantly filling up the guest rooms, draining the liquor cabinets, using tons of towels and leaving long after their welcome was worn out.

Though her part of the social calendar was cut back, William seemed to keep his four tuxedoes in and out of the dry cleaners with interesting regularity. She could have worn the same black velvet dress to every party and no one would have been the wiser.

Somehow she got through the season and was actually looking forward to January. With all the snow and cold wind off the lake, Cleveland had it's own beauty and she loved walking on the few sunny days they were afforded. But walking alone was not sufficient for her soul and Patti began to think about her future. Long ago someone told her, *be careful what you pray for, you might get it.* She had prayed for a beautiful life, and though it was cast with a *Cinderella* aura, she was not happy. The ball, the coach, even the mice, it was not what she had dreamed. The price was too high and she must find a way out. A way to get away from people, people, and people.

CHAPTER NINE

THE DECISION... to make a break and try life alone struck Patti one day in the third year of their marriage as she was driving to her fourth luncheon in a week.

"I would rather be reading a good book, planting a garden, painting a picture, or just plain listening to the wind. The way of life here is measured by how many designer dresses you own, how many holiday invitations you received, how many promotions your husband's received in the past six months, where you are going on your next cruise, and when do you have your next plastic surgery scheduled."

Adding to this was that mess with Perry Kessler. It was more overwhelming than she could take and was beginning to manifest itself in strange ways. She slept fitfully, ate little, had lost a lot of weight, and experienced periods of terrible depression. Realizing she just didn't fit in this scene, Patti picked up the telephone and called a travel agency... not the one William used for his business travel and their pleasure trips. She called Holiday Hits near the office where she had worked and spoke to Jennifer.

"Hello, I'm interested in flying to London and would like some quotes on rates."

"When do you want to leave and return?" Jennifer asked.

"Probably in a month or so and I'm only interested in one way... just getting there," Patti replied with a shaky courage in her voice.

After getting the requested information and deciding on a flight, she told the agent that she would stop by to pick up the ticket and brochures. Delivery to the house would never do.

A friend once told her about a lovely English village called Kersey. She had totally forgotten about it until the kind priest she met in Dublin said that was where he lived. Kersey was northeast of London by about fifty miles and easily accessed by train from Liverpool Station to Sudbury and then a local taxi to this picturesque village, as described by her friend. Kersey had a population of less than one hundred people, two pubs, one pottery, one general store, a weaver's cottage, and a small stone church at the top of the hill which also housed the local school. "Perhaps this was the reverend's church," she thought, "There's probably only one in a village so small."

The village was split by a dark running stream and spillway on the road, into which the local duck population chose to swim and preen themselves with no heed to the occasional car passing through. Nestled in Constable country, Kersey sounded exactly like the place she could "run and hide... even though they say you can't."

Now she remembered. They had passed through Kersey on a business trip some months ago to Lavenham where a World War II air museum is housed and where William hoped to acquire interest in exchanging parts for some antique airplanes in which he had an interest… one of the many hobbies he shared with his friends. On this particular trip William chose to rent a car and drive, rather than hire a taxi. They took the A134 toward Lavenham, but somewhere along the road took the wrong fork and wound up in Kersey. Stopping briefly at the pub for directions and a glass of ale, Patti noticed the calm and peace that seemed to emit from this small village. Not one to linger for things of the soul, William said they had to press on and her picture of Kersey would have to be forever stashed away for safekeeping in her heart.

"Yes," she thought, "that is where I'll go." Now she wished she had gotten the reverend's name so that she would have at least one contact when she arrived.

"Oh well, not to worry. I can find him when I get to Kersey."

The next few days she spent making mental and written lists of the things she wanted to take with her and those she wanted to get over to the Meads before any of the North's suspected anything. It would not be wise to tell anyone, even the Meads, that she was leaving the country. But she knew she would need some excuse for bringing all of those boxes to their house. I can always tell them we are redecorating and I just want to store some stuff for a while. As she went through her closets and drawers, she sadly identified each article of clothing or jewelry with a special event where she had hoped she and William would have a good time. But each occasion seemed to turn into a shouting match with William criticizing her for any number of things... "You spend too much time with too few people," "Why did you wear that same dress to their house?" "Can't you tell the cook to make a better salad?"

"How can you expect to help the business if you only talk about..." on and on, until she felt she would never be able to please him. All Patti wanted to do was be herself and apparently that was not good enough for him.

"Why had he changed so? Ever since that first night alone in the cabin, he's been a person of many moods."

She had a hard time keeping up with which mood would be present each day. Finally she quit trying and just tried to stay out of his way, do the best she could to please him, and find her own gratification in books and nature.

Choosing a few sets of clothes, mostly skirts and sweaters, she packed with great care, giving detail to bringing only the dire necessities. "I can always buy what I need when I get there." With the remainder of her parents' insurance money and some she had saved from her job, she felt it would be possible to live comfortably for a few months while she looked for work. Patti made up her mind to live a simple life, using her resources only for shelter and food. Walks in the English mist and a good book with a cup of tea would be her pleasures now. The thought of this brought a smile to her face, one of few seen there lately.

Patti had chosen May sixth as the day to leave. It was a Thursday and that would bring her in to London on Friday morning. As the days drew closer, she was daily getting a sick feeling in her stomach, wondering if this was truly the right thing to do, or was she being selfish. One evening at dinner, Marian questioned her lack of appetite.

"Patti, lately you hardly touch your food and you look so pale. Why don't you go up to the cabin for a few days and sit in the sun on the dock. The change might help and you can give me some ideas while you're there on how to change the furniture around in the great room. It's starting to look tired."

This could be just the excuse for leaving that she needed.

"I'll think about that, Mother North. I have some hospital meetings this month, but maybe early next month I could take a few days," she said with a definite lilt to her voice.

Looking around, she noticed that they were all, including William, surprised at her accepting attitude.

Patti had been very cautious in keeping her bags hidden. The house staff rarely looked deep into her closets, at least she hoped they didn't. But just seeing two suitcases wouldn't cause alarm. Anyway, now she could do it in the open since she was *going to the cabin in early May.* She took great delight in roaming the aisles of the local pharmacy, finding small travel sizes of shampoo, deodorant, and other items she would need until she became acquainted with her new shopping places. Since London was not far from Kersey, it might be fun to take the train in once in a while and do more serious buying. These thoughts gave Patti a new and joyful reason for facing each day. The future was starting to look bright, through the mist and to the hills.

Realizing that it would not take long to find her whereabouts once it was discovered that she did not go to the cabin, Patti felt she must leave a letter for William. She did not blame him for all of her unhappiness. He did what he felt was best for him and some of the time that included her. She knew she could not change him, only wished she had known who he really was before she fell into the *Cinderella* trap. This was what she had to do and it had to be in her way. So, she sat down at her Queen Anne desk and started the letter.

Dear William,

By the time you read this, I will be on my way to England and may have already landed in London. The past three years have been the most challenging of my entire life. Entering into our marriage with complete faith and love for you, I find that I do not really know you and don't think I ever will. Please don't think that I blame you for my unhappiness. I have tried to adapt to this life, but it is too complicated for me and I should have seen that long ago. It's not fair to you to be joined to one who cannot adjust to what you see as important in life. The presence of so many people in our daily lives has just become too much for me to endure. I tried so many times to let you know that I wanted to be alone with you, but there were always other people who came first. Don't worry about me, I'll take care of myself and will hopefully find the peace and contentment that I so desperately need. I'll write to you in time, but please don't try to find me. I am not running away, I am running to.

With love,

Patti

As she sealed the envelope, she began to cry and knew that she did not want to ever hurt him. He was as good to her as he could be. William was just William. A product of the "more" syndrome, it was not his fault that he did not have the compassionate feelings to share that she craved. Guess it would have been fine if she was like one of "those bimbos". Patti knew it was too late now to change William or herself and she could only continue with her plan.

The coordination of this *getaway* was becoming more complicated than she had anticipated. How was she going to get to the airport when they thought she would be driving her car to the cabin at Geneva-on-the-Lake? Patti pensively speculated on this for a few minutes and decided she would drive her car to the Meads and take a taxi from there. They would both be at work and wouldn't discover the car until long after she had taken off for London. At least the car would be safe, Dad Mead would see to that, and if William wanted it back he could come and get it. Dad Mead wouldn't object and cause any problems. She thought she better leave a letter for them, too. After all, they were the only *family* she really felt close to since her parents died. They had always stuck by her and supported her choices. She knew they would understand and be with her on this decision as well. Carefully wording the letter she told them she needed to do this for her own sanity and had no intention of hurting William or anyone else. She let them know that they were very special to her and she would be in touch, but not to worry for the time being.

On the chosen day, Patti awakened feeling more refreshed than she had in months. She felt a glowing and happy presence in her soul. This was most curious because the night before William had insisted they stay late at a dinner party. Thinking about all she had to face the next day, she had hoped to be able to leave early. When they arrived home he became quite amorous and his tenderness to her was most contrary to his normal manner of making love. This night he seemed to be more aware of her and was extremely gentle. Turning off the bedside light, he kissed her tenderly on the cheek and said, "Fair Lady, I may not be the Knight you were seeking, but I do love you in my own way. Don't ever forget that."

"William, I, I," crying, she wanted so badly to tell him she was leaving, but it was too late. Instead, she put her arms around his firm, tanned chest and hugged tight. "It'll be alright, I know it will," she told herself.

****

Marian gave her a hug comparable to one you would give to a porcupine, and then watched her load her luggage into the trunk of the car. Patti was afraid she would ask why she was taking her good luggage instead of the canvas logo bags she usually took to the lake.

Fortunately, at that moment a truck with flowers for the Friday night dinner arrived and took her attention. Patti turned the car around in the circular drive and waved as she turned on to the road. A sense of pure freedom filled her head as she took a deep breath of the cool air blowing in from Lake Erie.

Pulling in to the driveway at the Meads, Patti was careful to get as far back from the street as possible. She knew the neighborhood had not improved and the sight of a nice, shiny coupe like hers would only tempt certain people. She hoped Dad Mead would call William right away, so he could come and get the car. But then, wondering to herself, she thought, "Why do I care? It's just a car and another of the *things* that trapped me." Finding her key to the back door, she opened the screen door and inserted the key. Once inside the kitchen, she quickly dialed the taxi company and asked for a taxi to the airport. Ten minutes later a yellow cab pulled into the driveway and the driver loaded her bags into the trunk.

As they came up the ramp to the departure area, Patti thought about their wedding day and the trip to this same airport for their honeymoon starting in New York. She would be taking part of that same route, except she would land and change planes at JFK airport instead of LaGuardia before proceeding to Gatwick Airport, south of London. She paid the driver, followed the skycap to check in her luggage and walked down the concourse to her American Airlines gate. She originally had thought of taking the Concorde over, but knew the cost would dig too deeply into her carefully guarded stash. "I must be practical and save all I can."

The flight attendant called for boarding, and Patti, picking up her carry-on bag, followed the others who were sitting in coach. "Oh, dear God, I do hope I have made the right decision, but it was the only choice I had. Please guide me and let me find some peace," she prayed as she stepped into the wide-bodied jet. "I'm on my way."

CHAPTER TEN

THE FLIGHT OVER... would turn out to be longer than she had expected, but probably was due to her anxiety of being found before departure. Patti's carefully prepared note to William was certain to be found by now and she wondered how he was reacting. She also thought about the Meads and how they would handle this unexpected happening in their otherwise quiet lives. She hoped they would not be sad, but happy that she had chosen to make a difference in her life. She could almost hear Marian telling William that she "never felt that girl would fit into our lifestyle".

"Well, she was right about that," Patti thought as she vividly recalled the past three years. "And at this moment I don't even care."

She did not yet know that her future was going to change so drastically, not only because of her new surroundings, but also because of the people she would meet and their expectations and apprehensions of her move to this strange little village, Kersey. Somehow the unknown made her feel excited and without the fear she earlier had dreaded in making this choice.

As the flight attendant passed through the aisle with glasses of water and orange juice, Patti had a slight feeling of nausea and wondered if her anxiety was catching up with her. The elderly lady sitting in the window seat was engrossed in reading her "Upper Room" magazine, giving Patti the suggestion that she might best say another prayer or two that she had made a wise decision. She asked for guidance in this terribly daring venture and hoped it was His will that she be on this plane.

"Too late now." The plane was rolling down the runway ready to leave Cleveland Hopkins Airport. "Next stop, Gatwick London Airport, UK."

Just as she was finding a comfortable position in the small coach seat, and remembering the luxury of traveling in first class with William, the flight attendant announced that they would be serving dinner and then turn on the movie. Patti did not really feel like eating, but knew she had a hectic twelve or so hours ahead of her and would need the strength. Airline food was not the kind you fill up on anyway, so there was no chance of her feeling stuffed. She even considered another glass of champagne to match the one she had just finished. This seemed to calm her nerves a bit, and with the warmth of the airline issue wool blanket, she started to settle down and feel ready for a nap.

"Maybe dinner will have to wait."

Drifting into a state of dreamy euphoria, she began to have a vision of being in a dark, high-walled courtyard. The top of the wall was higher than she could reach without something on which to stand and there was nothing to climb on… not even rocks. The courtyard was void of all objects and was covered by a dark cloud that hung deep into the open space. She heard no noises, the air was still. In her dream she began to scream and wail.

"Where am I? Help me get out, please, somebody."

She found a small crack in the base of the wall and started to dig with vigor akin to a trapped animal. With bleeding fingers, she scratched at the rock structure and was beginning to make a minute hole in the wall. Just as she noticed a bit of daylight from the other side, someone tapped her on the shoulder.

"Are you ready for your dinner, ma'am?" asked the flight attendant. Patti jumped at the sound of her voice.

"Oh, thank you. Yes, guess I was dreaming." She sat up, dropped the tray table down in front of her, and watched as the lady next to her gave a quizzical stare.

"Perhaps I was crying out loud. Was this a vision of my escape from the past?" she asked herself, struggling to regain entry into wakefulness.

The meal was as interesting and inviting as if it had been one from a Barbie doll playhouse. The chicken and rice was tough and cold with a greasy gravy unsuccessfully garnished with pimientos. Green beans that left the vine several weeks ago were overcooked and highly salted. The limp salad could not be revived with the lemon vinaigrette dressing and the rolls were only exceeded in taste by the bitter chocolate pie with fake whipped cream. After a few tastes of each, Patti went back to sipping her champagne and looked forward to a nice cup of hot tea. This would get her started on what would become her favorite drink of the day. "Didn't all English folk like their *cuppa?*"

The more she thought about this great adventure, the more excited she became, as she contemplated all of the decisions and arrangements that lay ahead. For weeks Patti had meticulously entered notes and ideas about what she had to do into a small booklet kept hidden in the bottom of her cedar chest. She knew there was no chance of William going in there. He had no interest in her possessions, or her thoughts for that matter. How she wished he would have wanted to share more of her dreams. The booklet was now in the bottom of her carry-on bag and she reached to find it and start her mind moving on some definite plans once she arrived in London.

It would be necessary to stay the first night in London and then catch an early morning train to Colchester and Sudbury. She had heard of a small South Kensington hotel, *The Tramore*. A former townhouse, it had only ten rooms and her travel agent said it was moderately priced. Within walking distance of the museums, bookstores, and small, ethnic restaurants, even *Christie's* was in the next block, should she want to take a peek. Though that could be risky, in case any of William's contacts were there. "I might stay a couple of days to gather my thoughts and make some inquiries about rentals in Kersey." She knew the London agencies handled rentals for the entire of Great Britain.

The precious booklet, her passport to her new life, listed several agencies and she mentally noted two that she would call tomorrow morning. Fortunately, they were both located in the Kensington area and since she planned to do a lot of walking, that excursion would be on her list of things to do first. All of this anticipation was beginning to spin in her head and she decided it might be wise to try and sleep, if only for a few hours. Actually, it would be only a few hours and then they would serve breakfast prior to landing.

Sleep became a contest. Each time she drifted off she went back into the courtyard nightmare. Rousing herself and trying to find some rest without the dream, she was aware that her seatmate was becoming irritated with her restlessness.

"I'm sorry," she said to the little grey haired lady, "I keep having a bad dream."

Smiling, the lady said, "Why don't you try thinking about something very happy and maybe you will be able to sleep."

With that grandmotherly advice, she turned her head to the window and leaned on her pillow.

Finally lapsing into sleep without dreams, for what seemed to be only a few minutes, she was awakened by the flight attendant offering her a hot towel. Knowing that breakfast would be next, Patti decided it was useless to attempt to sleep more. She went back to the bathroom in the rear of the plane and tried to freshen her makeup and straighten her hair from the mess it had become. It was bumpy in the back of the plane and she started to feel a bit queasy.

As she got into her seat, she saw the breakfast cart a few seats away and realized she really wanted a nice, hot, cup of coffee. This meal didn't look as unpalatable as dinner and she was quite hungry by now. On her tray was a box of cereal, box of milk, carton of strawberry yogurt, fresh orange slices and a warm scone… yes, warm, with a big pat of butter. It did not take long for her to finish her breakfast and she then enjoyed sitting back and sipping the coffee.

Almost as soon as the last of the breakfast trays had been gathered, the first officer was announcing their approach into Gatwick. Looking out the window, Patti sighed as she saw the neat green patches of farms with what looked like dots of white. Those dots were the many sheep that supplied the main meat source for Great Britain and other parts of Europe. Puffy, white clouds seemed to float between the plane's altitude and the ground. The sun was starting to rise and its rays were reflected in the many ponds throughout the countryside. Only three a.m. back in the States, it was eight a.m. in London and cars were lining all of the roads leading into the busy city, taking workers to the many places of commerce that made this one of the great and thriving cities of the world. From high in the sky, the cars looked like little toys and the occasional thatched roof houses appeared as broom topped boxes. Winding lanes were bordered by rows and rows of hedges, all as boundaries of land.

Hearing the heavy metal sound of the landing gear being lowered, Patti checked to be sure her bags were secured and her seat belt fastened. She opened her handbag for a last look to be sure her passport was handy. Knowing that she would need some local currency for tips and taxis, she had exchanged a hundred dollars at the airport. This gave her 65 British pounds, the exchange rate not being the best today. She took several pounds out and put them in her coat pocket...a pocket in the ever-ready trench coat that would become like a second skin in the months to come.

The landing was smooth and she was glad to be sitting fairly close to the front for easy exit. Still, she and the *grandmother* had to wait several minutes before they stepped on to the jet way that lead to the gates and then to immigration. On what seemed like ten miles of moving sidewalk, they made their way to the immigration room. As the sidewalk took them to their destination, they passed posters advertising strong European cigarettes, current theater productions, fancy flavored candies, and expensive Scottish single blend whiskey. There were also large posters warning passengers to keep their personal belongings with them at all times. Security was far more prevalent overseas than at home. Perhaps this was due to the recent increase in terrorism. Patti read every poster, and stepping off the last section of sidewalk, made her way to the escalator that went down to immigration. She tried to find the shortest line and took her passport out, ready for inspection.

The agent asked her where she would be staying, how long she would be in the country, and the nature of her visit. To the last question she answered, "to visit friends.", because she still was not sure of her ensuing problems in staying here to work. If it was anything like in the States, she knew she was in for trouble. Passing through the turnstile, she went down still another long hallway to the baggage claim area. Passing through the *"nothing to claim"* aisle in the Customs hall, she entered the large waiting part of the terminal. Lined with coffee shops, newsstands, exchange counters, and thousands of people, the doors to the outside were hardly visible. Looking up she saw a directional sign to the *taxi rank* ... taxi stand. She was most grateful for the large luggage carts that were supplied by the government at no cost to the passengers. With her two large bags and one carry-on bag loaded securely, she pushed her cart out to the sidewalk and started toward a waiting black taxi.

"No," she thought to herself, "I will not spend the money on a taxi all the way in to London. I'll find the train and take that." So, turning around, she reentered the terminal, found a uniformed airport guard and asked for directions to the train.

A man of about fifty, dressed in typical English tweed, offered to lift her bags into the train. Thanking him, she found a seat near the front and was pleased when he asked if he could join her. "Yes, that would be fine," she answered with a smile.

"Are you here on holiday, miss?"

"Yes", she meekly replied, "I am going to visit in the Suffolk area."

"You are in for a treat then," he said. "That's Constable and Gainsborough country and if you like art you shall have a lot to see. In fact Gainsborough's house is in Sudbury, and if you get near there it is open for visitation."

They both bought tea from the host as he passed the refreshment cart through the car. The man dozed and Patti looked out the window as they passed through small communities surrounding London. She could see the back yards of houses where almost every family had a garden with roses. Mixed among the clothes lines and the toppled outdoor aluminum furniture were toys of all description and piles of lumber waiting to be used for the next project. Here and there lights could be seen in a kitchen behind the lace-curtained windows, but for the most part the homes looked dark. By now the inhabitants were probably on their way to work and school. It was almost ten thirty and she was really beginning to feel the effects of no sleep. She thought how good it would be to take a nice, hot bubble bath in one of those deep English bathtubs and then a long, delicious nap.

"Perhaps there will be a *Boots* pharmacy near the hotel where I can buy some bath oil and bubble bath."

On a previous trip with William she had bought some that had a rose fragrance and permeated their whole suite. She loved it. He said it smelled like a funeral home.

The train pulled into Victoria Station and once again she put all of her bags on a cart, though by now they felt as if she had loaded them with heavy rocks. Walking to the front of the terminal, she got into the taxi rank and waited her turn for one of the shiny, black taxis that were so symbolic of English travel. The driver, apparently not one to talk much, asked where she wanted to go and did not utter another word until he turned onto Cranley Place and stopped in front of Number 10 and *The Tramore*. She paid the £4 fare and gave him a more than generous tip considering his lack of communication. But just as well, because she felt too tired to talk, too.

As she approached the reception desk, which was just that, a nice antique desk with a few papers and a vase of tulips, a pretty girl with long red hair came to her and attempted to help her with the bags.

"Thank you, they're not too heavy, but I will need help with them to my room."

"May I have your name?" the girl asked as she opened a large leather-bound book, which was obviously the guest register.

"No computerization here," Patti silently noted.

"I'm Patti North and my travel agent in Cleveland made my reservation. I was wondering if it would be possible to stay an extra day or two?"

"Oh, not a problem, ma'am. Just sign here and I'll be showin' you to your room."

Patti filled in her name and saw that she was being assigned room Number 350.

Reaching for one of the bags, the girl said, "You're going to be on the third floor, ma'am, and I'm sorry but there's no lift here. You'll have to take the stairs, but a mite o' exercise is good for the soul." At this point Patti was so tired that three floors or ten floors really didn't make a difference.

As they entered the room, she knew this was perfect. The bed looked reasonably firm, the armoire would more than accommodate the few clothes she had brought and the tub was indeed deep. Adding to her instant feeling of peace, Patti noticed the fireplace and the small table and chairs by the window that overlooked a garden in the neighbor's yard. Situated on one of the many *mews,* the adjacent house had a slate roof and benches among the rose bushes.

She thanked the girl for her help, opened her bags, found her toothbrush and went into the blue and white bathroom. Turning on the water to fill the tub, she added the sample size bath gel from the amenity basket and watched the bubbles form. A knock at the door snapped her out of her euphoric daze and she almost tripped on the bedspread as she rushed to see who could be there. Looking through the peephole, she saw the girl from reception holding a silver tray with a small crystal bottle of brandy, two glasses, and a large white envelope. She opened the door and taking the tray from the girl, she said, "Thank you, but who sent this?"

"Oh ma'am, the manager wants to welcome you and asked me to extend his invitation to you to dine with him tonight."

"The manager? I don't even know him, or you. By the way, what is your name?"

"My name is Maureen and the manager is Colin Wadsworth. He saw you checking in and noticed that you were alone. Please don't take offense. He's a very proper man, he is, and only wants to be hospitable."

Patti stood there staring at the polite girl, and looking at the envelope, said," I must get some rest before I can even think about this. Please tell Mr. Wadsworth thank you and I'll respond later today if that's suitable."

As she shut the door, she took the envelope from the tray and turning it over saw the large initials, CCW. Inside, written in rather large script, was a note from Colin C. Wadsworth, welcoming her to the *Tramore* and asking her to join him and *two other new guests* in the dining room downstairs at seven. With a sigh of relief she laid the envelope down, went into the bathroom and took off her well traveled clothes. Sinking into the steaming hot water, she laid back her head and started to dream of tomorrow.

CHAPTER ELEVEN

TRYING TO BE QUIET… William crept up the back stairs of the mansion and tiptoed down the rear hall to his and Patti's quarters. It was two a.m. Originally meant for additional staff apartments, the North's had redecorated extensively and turned this part of the house into a *home* for the newlyweds. With three large bedrooms and baths, it also had a living room, small dining area and kitchen and a sun porch spanning the entire back width of the building. Most of their meals were taken with the rest of the family, so the dining and kitchen facilities were rarely used except for morning coffee or Patti's afternoon tea. Decorated in Marian's favorite pastels, Patti would like to have had brighter colors, at least in some of the furniture fabric and window dressings. Since she was not consulted, and felt grateful to have this lovely home, it seemed best to make do and enjoy the comfort of such luxury.

Reaching gingerly for the curved brass doorknob, William was surprised to find it was not locked. As he turned the handle and stepped inside, he was also aware that Patti had not left the lamp lit on the foyer table as she usually did when he was to be out late. Thinking that perhaps the bulb had burned out, he nevertheless tried to turn it on. Much to his amazement, it came on. "Guess she forgot," he thought as he walked on through to their bedroom, trying to be as quiet as possible, while fully expecting to trip over something.

He found his way into his bathroom, which was separated by a sitting area from Patti's private bath. Turning on the light, he began to undress. Noting that the doors were open through the sitting area... Patti always closed these at night to keep his light out of her eyes... he walked in and found the light switch for their bedside lamps. Then he remembered. "She's at the lake." In his slightly inebriated state he had forgotten that Patti was going to the cabin for a few days rest and would not have been here to leave a light on for him.

The bed was still made, the quilted spread intact, pillows in their places, and no Patti. On his pillow was an ivory envelope with the familiar *PHN* initials on the top left corner.

Thinking it was probably one of her notes to say she would miss him... "She'd only be gone four days"... he tossed it on the chair next to the bed and pulled down the quilt. The late evening of dinner with his friends and a lengthy poker game mixed with too many scotches were catching up with him. All he wanted to do was sleep, not read sugary notes.

The next morning, after sleeping until eleven, he dressed in his golf clothes, and as he breezed through the kitchen to grab a bagel and a cup of coffee, he heard his mother coming into the room.

"Dear" she said in a smotherly tone, "if you talk to Patti today, please ask her to measure the living room windows for me. I want to order new drapes and can't find my old notes on the cabin."

"Mom, you can call her. I have an important lunch meeting and then a game with the guys. Won't have time to call her," he replied as he went out the back door to the garage.

The lunch meeting was short, with the customer deciding almost immediately to buy the new North purchase, one of Jamie Wyeth's pig pictures. The pig paintings were unique and sold well. William had secured this one from a gallery in Greenville, South Carolina that specialized exclusively in works of all the Wyeths. Shaking hands and offering thanks, both men watched as the valet brought the man's car through the portico. William walked back down the side of the main building and into the golf pro shop where his three friends were waiting.

"You're late, buddy, our tee time is right now," one of them called out to him as he went into the locker room to put on his shoes. A few minutes later they had teed off and were headed down the fairway to number two tee, oblivious to the trials and tribulations of daily commerce.

Since he had no real reason to get home early, William decided to accept one of his friend's invitation to go to a local strip joint after a quick dinner at the club. He had not indulged in this sort of activity since college days and it sounded like a fun thing to do. "Who would know?" He had a vague feeling of missing Patti, but it passed quickly and he focused on the pleasure awaiting.

They drove downtown and turned into one of the side streets near the Square. With it's flashing neon sign of a shapely girl, the doorway of the club bid their entrance for an interesting evening. Inside was clouded with smoke and the blaring sounds of gyrative music seemed to make the old wooden floor shake. At the far end of the crowded room was a small stage with several ceiling to floor poles. Around each pole a girl was giving movement to the music while at the same time shedding various items of garish costume.

William, and his friend, George, found a table near the side of the stage and when the highly painted waitress asked for their order, they both chose scotch. The watered down drinks were insignificant to the show that kept their attention. Each of the exotic dancers had started out in a costume representing a jungle animal and during the course of the act they not only stripped, but also tried to create an interactive scene among themselves. Their weak attempts at imitating the animals was hardly noticed by the glaring men who seemed to find intense and abundant gratification in this limp display of an old art.

William seemed to be in deep concentration as he stared at a tall, buxom, redhead dressed... or formerly dressed... as a zebra. She was by now down to a very tiny bra and thong in a sheer black and white striped fabric. Undoubtedly one of the least skilled in dancing, she smiled a lot and blinked her eyes with undue rapidity, but hardly offered any dance movements other than her sensuous attachment to the pole. As the music came to an end, her eyes met William's and she shrieked, "Hey, good lookin! Where you been?"

"Oh my word," he thought. It was Paula Stratamondi, the boisterous gal one of his friends brought to the club when he and Patti were first dating. Last he heard she had gone to New York to find her fortune on *The Great White Way*. "Guess she didn't make it." Thinking it might be wise to leave right away, he jumped up, grabbed George's sleeve and said, "Let's get outa here NOW."

Before they could make it to the door, Paula had caught up with them. Totally unaware of her state of dress, she threw her arms around his neck and gave him a big, wet kiss. He stepped back, pushed her away, causing her to fall over a nearby chair. At that moment a huge man lunged at William and threw him to the floor. George, not wanting to be in this fracas, ran out the front door, leaving William to fend for himself. William got up, told the bouncer there was some mistake and that he didn't know this girl, stuffed several bills in the man's shirt pocket and made his way to the door and the welcome cool of the night.

George had brought his car around to the front of the building, and reaching over to open the door for him, said, "Sorry I ducked out, but if my wife ever found out about me being here, I'd be in court real fast."

William didn't even care about what Patti might think, his only concern right now was getting back to Shaker Heights. He did, however, cogitate for a few moments on the physical attributes of Paula Stratamondi.

George pulled in to the parking area at the Vandermere where William had left his car, and told him he was sorry their night on the town was such a bust. "Maybe next time we can find a place where you don't know the dancers. Ha, ha."

As he parked his car in the dark garage, William could see lights burning in his parent's living room. Deciding to stop and talk with them for a few minutes, he hoped he would not get the third degree questioning for which Marian was well known when he was younger. Much to his pleasant surprise, they made no reference to his whereabouts that evening, but his mother did tell him she got no answer at the cabin that afternoon when she tried to call Patti.

"Don't worry," William said as he fixed himself a scotch from their very elaborate and well-stocked bar. "She was probably out on the dock or taking a walk around the lake paths. I'll try her when I go upstairs. What was it you wanted her to do again?"

She refreshed his mind about the window measurements and told him to ask Patti to write it down with some drawings, if possible. He finished his drink, gave his mother a whisk of a kiss on the cheek, told his dad goodnight, and proceeded up to the apartment.

Once inside the apartment, he undid his tie and pulling it from his collar, walked over to the bedside chair and picked up the note from Patti.

Dear William,

By the time you read this, I will be on my way to England...

... I am not running away, I am running to.

With love,

Falling into the chair, he read the letter several times, shaking his head and starting to feel emotions of anger and rage.

"How could she leave me? How could she leave all this? How could she be so stupid and selfish?" The more he questioned, the more furious and incensed he became. Standing up with a jerk, he reached for a Beleek vase they had bought in Dublin and hurled it across the room to the wall. It crashed into tiny pieces.

"I'll find her. I'll bring her back and make her sorry she ever left."

A knock on the door snapped him into reality.

"Come in."

"William, what was that noise? Are you alright?" Marian asked as she stood there looking at him.

"She's not at the lake, Mother. She's flown to London. Why, I don't know and she did not say where she was staying."

All of a sudden, feeling like a hurt little boy, he put his arms around his mother and started to sob. She picked up the note and read the contents.

"How could she do this? What did I do to make her want to leave?"

"Don't blame yourself, dear. She has not been happy here and you did nothing to make her leave," Marian said, as she delighted in the feeling of William needing her now as he used to long ago. "Go to bed and tackle this in the morning. You can't do anything about it tonight and obviously she doesn't want to be found, so don't be so concerned." He suddenly and silently questioned his mother's cool aloofness to the situation.

"Maybe a good night's rest will clear my head and I'll be able to find some plan to settle this. You're right, Mother, it doesn't sound like she wants to be found."

Just as she had so many times in the past, Marian tucked him in to bed, kissed him on the forehead and left the room. He felt like he was a ten year old little boy, but with a bruised ego of a grown man. For almost three years he had been the one in this marriage to call the shots. Now Patti had countered and succeeded in reducing him to tears… something no one had done since his last schoolboy fight. His resentment would be something for all of them to reckon with. Compassion and understanding were not part of the North legacy.

"I'll worry about this tomorrow, but not until I call my lawyer. No woman can get away with making any North look foolish." And so he went to sleep.

Marian stopped at the door, turned to take another look at her sleeping child, and began to reflect on the past few years. "Funny, I never felt comfortable with that girl. She was bright and pretty, but it seemed she harbored a dark resentment within her spirit. None of us were able to get her to open up and truly be a part of our lifestyle. Guess coming from such a dismal background one could not expect her to be socially adroit."

Slowly and quietly easing into one of the soft sitting room chairs, Marian took a lace-edged handerchief from her robe pocket and gently wiped the tears from her eyes. "I did try to love that girl, but it was a constant struggle to make her accept our ways. Even if William was more involved with his friends than with her, she could have found activities to keep busy. I did." Her thoughts ran back to when she and *her* William were courting. "Oh, the wonderful, wonderful parties with all of Cleveland's best families. I loved every minute of it… what a special time we had. Patti could have had this, too, if only she would have tried."

Thinking back on those early years of her marriage and William's birth, she also resented all the people intruding on his young life. He once told his mother, "I'll be glad when I'm grown up so I can run away from all these people." Often when the house was full of guests, he would retreat to his room and read books about foreign lands. "Curious that now it is Patti who has fled to another country to escape exactly what William used to say he hated." At some point in high school he changed. She never figured it out, how or why, but he suddenly started to join in all the social festivities and gathered about himself a large clan of friends and admirers. "Perhaps he realized we could not change and by then he knew someday he would inherit the family fortune with all the responsibilities of personal and civic duties. Resignation? I wonder," she thought as she heard him snoring in the next room.

Marian straightened the front of her robe across her ample bosom and tightening the belt, left the suite. In the downstairs kitchen she poured a glass of skim milk and took it back to her bedroom.

As she turned out the bedside light, feelings of sadness swept through her mind. "Just when I was getting used to the idea that becoming a grandmother might be nice, this happens. Oh well, all things for the best. William is young, he'll find someone more like us and we'll continue on."

CHAPTER TWELVE

THE SOUND OF BIRDS… chirping below in the neighbor's trees, woke her up. She rolled over, looked through the window, and saw that it was beginning to get dark outside. She remembered that the manager had asked her to join him and the other new guests for dinner. Wondering what time it was, she jumped out of the warm bed and tried to find her travel clock in her bag. She would have to dress quickly, as it was six thirty and they were expecting her at seven. Realizing she had not responded to the invitation, she picked up the telephone and called down to reception.

"Maureen, this is Mrs. North. I just woke up and apologize for calling so late. Does my invitation still stand to dine with Mr. Wadsworth?"

'Yes ma'am. He will be expecting you in the dining room on the lower level lookin' out on to the garden. I'll tell him you're coming."

Patti sifted through her bags and wished she had hung up her clothes before she took that wonderful nap. She pulled out a navy blue knit dress and a plaid blazer.

"Guess this will do," she said as she put on her panty hose and thought about what jewelry to wear. She did not bring any jewelry of great value, leaving all the precious baubles William had given her in the safe deposit box back in Cleveland. She had some earrings and pearls the Meads had given her for graduation, and though they were not costly, they had great value to her and would look nice with her outfit. Slipping her feet into the one pair of dress shoes she had packed, she reached for her handbag and decided she'd best leave her passport and other papers locked in her suitcase.

The walk down the four flights of stairs to the lower level beneath reception made her heart race. She was by now fully awake from the nap and felt she could be congenial, at least for a couple of hours.

Entering the dining room, Patti noticed several people surrounding a tall, stately gentleman, who she supposed was the general manager. As she walked toward them, he turned, left the group, and holding out his hand to her, said, "You must be Mrs. North. We welcome you to the Tramore. Do come and let me introduce you to some others who have just joined us today."

His very warm smile lighted up a face of deep blue eyes and light brown hair. He was dressed in tweed slacks and a camel's hair jacket, and Patti wondered how the English stood these heavy clothes, even in the summer time.

"Mrs. North," he said as he started to introduce her to the others.

"Patti, please, Mr. Wadsworth."

"Only if you call me Colin," he said as he laughed. "This is Pamela and Richard Ward from Leeds and Beverly and Henry Preston from your country. Boston, as a matter of fact."

"How do you do," she said as she reached to shake their hands." I apologize for being a bit late, but it was so nice to take a nap after checking in. I really didn't sleep much on the flight over and guess it caught up with me."

Maureen passed among them with a tray of sherry in beautiful cut crystal glasses, which Patti felt must surely be Waterford, while Colin gave them a bit of history about the Tramore, telling them that it had been a private home for many years and two years ago an investor from Saudi Arabia had purchased and changed it into a hotel. The dining area had originally been the kitchen and sleeping quarters for the staff. Reception had been the family parlor and the sun porch on the back of first floor rooms was the playroom for the owner's children.

The Wards were in from Leeds on business. He was a banker calling on London banks regarding new banking laws. The Prestons from Boston came to London as part of a three-week holiday touring England, Ireland and Wales. They would be leaving with their tour group in a couple of days and wanted to spend some time in the city before their departure. Colin told them about the big market at

Portobello Road, northwest of Kensington. With hundreds of shops, outside carts and several pubs, the weekend Portobello Market was not only a tourist attraction, but was frequented by the citizens of the area as well. He said they could walk two blocks to the tube station, and taking the Circle line from the South Kensington station and exiting at Nottinghill Gate, they would only have a few blocks walk to the start of the market. Since it was only open on weekends, and she would be leaving by Monday, Patti thought it would be fun to try to go tomorrow and see what it was all about. She asked the other ladies if they were interested, but they both declined, stating other planned activities. "Well, I'll just go alone. Time I started to find my way around here anyway," she thought as she anticipated hunting for treasures she might need in her new adventure.

Maureen announced that dinner was to be served and they all took their seats, Colin holding Patti's chair as she smiled up at him. After a bowl of hot creamed squash soup, there was a mixed salad and then the entree of roasted lamb with baby carrots, new potatoes and freshly made mint sauce from the hotel's herb garden. Dessert of sherbet and cookies was followed by demitasse and an array of cordials over which Colin took delight describing. The after dinner conversation continued for about an hour when Patti rose and announced that she enjoyed the evening, but wanted to get a good night's rest so that she could tackle the market tomorrow. Thanking Colin for his hospitality, she turned to leave the room, when he gently took her arm and asked if she would like to take a short walk in the neighborhood before retiring.

"I really am tired, but it's so nice out tonight, perhaps that would be a good idea. Thank you, I'd love to take a walk."

"Good, let me say good night to the other guests and I'll join you in reception," he said, retreating back to the dining room.

They walked down the ten or so stone steps, out through the black iron gates, and on to the sidewalk of Cranley Place. Colin placed Patti's hand on his arm and asked her to tell him about herself and why she was in London. This intrusion into her privacy caught her as most remarkable, since she had always heard the English were more reserved and respectful of others' lives. But, somehow it did not come across as being nosey, just interested. She cautiously told him that she needed to get away from an unhappy marriage situation and came across to be alone and think for a while. This seemed to satisfy him and as they crossed over Old Brompton Road, he led her into a small coffee shop and patisserie. The glass cases were full of tempting delicacies and the smell of freshly brewed coffee wafted through the air and among the small table sets. They each chose an eclair type pastry and a cup of cappuccino. Hoping the coffee would not keep her awake, she nonetheless enjoyed every morsel of the sweet dessert and wondered why her appetite had picked up so much in the past few days.

"Now that you know about me, tell me about Colin Wadsworth," she said with coyness in her voice.

"Not much to tell, really. I went to hotel school in Switzerland, came back here and worked in several large hotels. Married a girl from Morocco who was working with me at the Dorchester and she became dissatisfied living here. We politely chose to dissolve the marriage and went our own ways. Don't know where the kind lady is today. A friend from Saudi told me about the renovation at the Tramore and suggested I call the owner who was looking for a manager. It's a lot simpler life than I had before, but affords me time to pursue some hobbies when I have time off."

"And, what might those hobbies be?" she questioned as they started to leave the sweet shop.

"I have always wanted to learn more about art history. Being close to so many museums helps with that research. And, I like to paint, so I put to practice some of the strategies I read about. Both of these activities keep me near the hotel. I have a small studio in my apartment on the fourth floor, so Maureen can always find me."

"This is most interesting and coincidental. I was an art major in college and worked for a while at a large gallery back home. We probably appreciate some of the same artists," she said with a gaiety in her voice that surprised even her. "Do you like the Victorian artists…Girtin, Grimshaw, Cottman?"

"My, yes, I do. We have several Grimshaws at a small gallery near here on Onslow Square. Would you have time before you leave to visit there with me?"

Noting a sense of urgency in his voice, she responded, "I was planning to spend most of tomorrow at Portobello Market, but perhaps Sunday afternoon. Oh yes, I want to attend church Sunday morning. Is there an Anglican church in the neighborhood?"

"St. Augustine's is about four blocks away on Queen's Gate."

They were almost at Number 10 and Colin had started to slow his pace. Turning to her and stopping, he looked into her eyes, took both of her hands in his, and said, "My dear Patti, we have only shared a few short hours, but I feel that you are a very special lady. So fair and fragile. I do hope you will find the answers you are seeking and will somehow not forget a new friend here."

A pounding in her heart caused her to take a deep breath. "You have been so kind, Colin. How could I forget such a memorable time on my first night here." She really didn't want to say more and give him reason to pursue. "We'd better get back, I have a busy day tomorrow and am quite tired."

As she shut the door of her room, she listened for his footsteps on the stairs that let her know he was going to his suite above. This had been a memorable evening, even if it did add to the present confusion in her heart. "I must not let my emotions detract me from my plans."

She finally unpacked her clothes, hanging them in the antique armoire. It had a pretty beveled mirror on the front and a shelf inside for her shoes. She remembered to pack two pair of *sensible* shoes like the English wear, knowing that she would be doing a significant amount of walking for a long time. She went over to the window and looked down at the garden below. It looked like the neighbors had had a party and were bidding good night to their guests, as several people were getting into cars. The moon was shining brightly and she decided to leave the flowered drapes open, letting in the rays of light. Opening the window a bit, she could smell the fragrance of blossoms from below. Patti brushed her teeth, took off her makeup and put on her nightgown. Easing herself into the cozy bed, she had another pang of nausea and concluded that two desserts and two coffees were the reason.

"I must start to limit myself with my eating. This heavy eating can become a nice habit and a hard one to break," she thought as she closed her eyes.

The next morning Patti awakened to the sound of the birds again and the sun shining into her room, making stripes of light on her bed and carpet. The clock showed nine and she was amazed that she had slept so late, as she usually rose by seven at home. She took another tub bath, using the last of the complimentary gel and resolved that she would find a *Boots* today where she could buy a supply of bath items. She dried herself with one of the oversized thirsty towels and put on her makeup. Finding her slacks and sweater in the armoire, she finished dressing and reminded herself that she would need to find an exchange if she intended to do any serious shopping today.

As she passed the reception door, Maureen was rearranging a large bouquet of flowers on the coffee table.

"Good Morning, Maureen. Is there a place to change money nearby?"

"Good mornin' to ya', Mrs. North. Yes, you'd be findin' one right next to the bookstore at the corner," she answered with a lilt in her voice. "Or, if you're a headin' to Portobello, there's one at the entrance road, though they might charge you a higher exchange rate."

"Great. Well, I'll be on my way and see you later. Oh, Maureen, if anyone should call here for me, please don't give any information, just take a name and number."

"Sure thing, ma'am. You be havin' a nice day now. Don't forget to have some fish 'n chips for your lunch," she laughed.

Patti walked up to Old Brompton Road and went into the exchange store. She put her little stash of money in the zippered part of her purse and headed east to the tube station. On the way she passed travel agencies, luggage stores, music shops, *Europa* (where she noted she could buy groceries), pubs, gift shops and *Christie's*. Here she looked straight ahead, afraid she might see a familiar face. At the entrance to the station she saw a flower vendor, resolving to buy a bouquet of tulips on her way home. "They will look so pretty on my little table in front of the fireplace," she thought, with a new feeling of doing her own decorating.

She figured out how to buy a tube ticket, inserted her pounds into the proper slot and, taking her ticket, found her way to the right track for the Circle Line. The tube maps on all of the walls at the station made it easy for her to follow the route. She joined others waiting beside the naked tracks and saw the light in the distance, denoting the arrival of the train. The doors slid open and she jumped on board, grabbing a strap to get her balance. The train was full and she surmised most of them must be going to market.

"Well, today I'll just be another citizen out doing my weekly shopping," she silently laughed to herself as the train pulled away from the station and made it's way a little south and then northeast toward Notting Hill. As they passed the Glouchester station she remembered that there was a big antique car fair at the hotel there and some of William's friends had mentioned being here to attend. A wave of fear passed as she hoped there would not be a terrible coincidence of meeting any of them.

The train pulled into the station, she saw signs saying *Notting Hill Gate* were on both sides of the walls and followed the departing masses as the doors of the train opened. Turning right out of the station, she again followed the same people, hoping they were all headed to the same destination… Portobello Market. She made the right decision, seeing signs giving directions to the market. As she turned down a side street, she saw a shop with interesting handmade garments in the window. All the jackets, skirts, bags, hats and other items were made of fancy quilted fabric, some with satin linings. Stepping inside she asked the young girl behind the counter, "Can you tell me the price of the jacket in the front window?"

"That jacket is £80, ma'am. Do you want to try it on?"

"Yes, thank you."

She put the bright jacket of many colors around her shoulders. The satin lining felt good.

"I'll take this." Proud of her first purchase, she envisioned wearing it with the navy knit dress or her black knit skirt. She knew she had to be practical and make little go far. This jacket would help stretch her wardrobe and still add interest to the otherwise drab selection she packed in haste.

As she turned the corner she could not believe the sight of so many shoppers jamming the streets. They were lined with small shops and arcades, most selling antique or collectible goods. In the middle of the streets were vendors of fruit, war paraphernalia, dolls, old books, and anything that would sell. At each corner of the six or so block area street entertainers gave forth with music, magic, trained monkeys, or mime. Also on all the corners were pubs offering brews of specific breweries and some free houses... those who could sell brew from any or all breweries.

Patti walked slowly, looked at every booth or shop. She bought some antique linen pillow cases, a chipped Waterford bud vase, and a set of coffee spoons. Feeling a little weak after two hours of this, she tried to find a seat in one of the pubs where she could order a lunch. She found a table with a couple who were smoking smelly cigarettes and drinking what looked like their fourth round of ales. They invited her to sit in the third and only unused chair and she thanked them. The waitress took her order of a Ploughman's lunch and a glass of white wine. The lunch was good and filling… a piece of crusty bread, hunk of white English cheddar, some pickle relish and a big pickled onion. She ate it all, drank the wine and stood up to find the counter to pay her bill. All of a sudden she felt totally weightless and the next moment found herself looking up at several staring faces. She had passed out. The manager pushed his way through the crowd.

"You okay, missy?"

"Yes, I think so. Guess all the walking and then the wine made me a little light headed. I'll be okay," she said softly as she let a man with a long beard help her up.

Patti made her way back to the tube station and thought the lack of regular sleep and her emotional state were responsible for these latest in unusual feelings. She leaned her head against the train window, oblivious of the dirt from greasy heads prior to hers, and closed her eyes. The ride back to South Kensington station was not far and before she knew it she was up and out the doors. As she climbed to the top of the station steps and out onto Cromwell and Onslow, she remembered the tulips. She chose a bouquet of deep pink ones, paid the old lady at the register and crossed the street to Old Brompton. "I

131

will be so glad to get back to my room, have a cup of tea, and take a nap."

She asked Maureen to send up a tray of tea, thanked her and checked to see if she had any messages.

"No, ma'am. But, I'll bring your tea 'round in a bit."

"So much for my big day at market," she laughed to herself.

CHAPTER THIRTEEN

THE TAPPING OF RAIN ... on the open windowsill greeted Patti as she awakened from a good sleep.

"Oh, now I won't be able to go to church unless I take a taxi," she thought with disappointment. It was only a four-block walk, but trying to get a taxi in this weather might be a problem. "Maybe I'll just take it easy this morning. I can have a little breakfast in the dining room and perhaps Maureen has the *Sunday Times* or some magazines I might borrow."

She dressed in a fresh pair of khaki slacks, deciding that jeans would not be appropriate for Sunday, and found a navy turtleneck shirt. The gold hoop earrings completed her look and she started toward the door when her telephone began to ring.

"Hello."

"Patti, this is Colin. Guess you see the rain, and I know you wanted to go to church. I would be glad to drive you there, if you'd like."

"Thank you, Colin, but think I'll not try to go this morning. But, I would like to go with you to the gallery this afternoon if the invitation is still open."

Almost before she could finish he said, "Yes, yes, by all means, that would be fine. I have a bit of bookwork to do with Maureen this morning and thought we could get a little lunch at one of the pubs and then go to the gallery. Shall I meet you in reception, say about twelve-thirty?"

"Colin, that will be fine. I look forward to the day," she answered and then placed the receiver back in the cradle.

The waiter in the dining room served her a breakfast of Irish porridge and heavy cream, toast with orange marmalade and a large pot of very hot tea. Finishing, she saw Maureen across the room and waved. As she was leaving the room, Maureen spoke.

"Good morning, to 'ya, Mrs. North. So sorry it is a rainin' today and not fit for walkin'.

"That's okay, I think it will suit me to spend the morning reading. Do you by chance have the *Times* or a few magazines?"

"Yes, you'll find a good selection in reception. Just be helpin' yourself and let me know if I can do anything for 'ya," she warmly responded.

Patti walked the flight up to reception and noticed outside the front door that the rain had started to come down harder. The sky was very dark and the rumble of thunder could be heard in the distance.

"A typical English day," she thought as she looked through the stack of magazines, choosing three to go with the big Sunday newspaper.

She sat on the loveseat in front of the fireplace, and had it been a bit cooler, would have started a fire. The paper's headlines told of another explosion in Ireland. "Those poor people, still fighting over religion after all these years." She read every section and took particular interest in the Estate Agents' listings, specifically those in Suffolk. Looking in her bag for the booklet with all of her precious notes, her hand touched the small photo album she had packed. With pictures of her deceased parents, the Meads and the North's, she flipped to the last plastic sleeve and gazed at the snapshot of William, one of her favorites of him. It was taken on their honeymoon somewhere in Ireland when they had stopped at a roadside pub for lunch. The bittersweet memories of their special time alone flooded her soul and she started to cry. "Oh, am I doing this for the right reasons?" Then the memories of all the people around them in Cleveland snapped her back into reality.

She opened the booklet to the section she had made for "Housing" and wrote down some of the listed addresses and telephone numbers.

"Wonder if I can call any of these today. I don't think the English are as particular about Sunday business as we are in the States." She picked up the telephone and dialed a number in Sudbury. It was to an

Estate Agent who had a gardener's cottage for lease in Kersey. From the ad it sounded just like what she was looking for... one bedroom, kitchenette, small parlor, bath and inside running water. "I would hope so," she laughed to herself as she waited for the call to go through.

"Charles Abbott here," came the crisp voice.

"Hello, I'm calling about your advertisement for the cottage in Kersey. Is it still available?" she asked.

"Yes, yes. Hardly ever have anybody who would be a wantin' a house way out there in Kersey," he answered.

"Can you tell me a little about the cottage and how much the lease would cost."

"Well, it's not been lived in for a few years. Old codger who was the gardener for the big house in front lived there and he died. It needs some paint and a bit 'o new furniture, but... did you say it's just you, missy?"

"Yes, I'm,... I'm here to do some research of the Suffolk area and thought Kersey would be a good place to live."

"Like I said, it's a bit in need o' cleanin' up, but we can do that for ya'. The lease would have to be for at least six months and it's £250 a month."

She quickly figured that would be about $400 dollars a month in American money. A bit more than she wanted to spend, but if it was the right place she would take it. There couldn't be that many places to rent in such a small village.

"Would it be possible to see it this Tuesday or Wednesday, sir?"

"'Spose so. What time you be wantin' to get in?"

Trying to collect her thoughts, she said, "Well, I'll be coming by train to Sudbury on Monday afternoon. I understand you can only get to Kersey by taxi or car."

"That's right. But my office is not far from the train station and I can pick you up and take you out there Monday. Won't take but about fifteen minutes to drive it."

"Oh, that would be wonderful. I'll call you from the train station. My name is Patti North and I'm staying in London this weekend at the Tramore. Thank you, Mr. Abbott."

"Right. See you on Monday," and he hung up.

She felt so happy to be making some progress on this exciting adventure. Her mind raced on with thoughts of having her very own little house... even if it was leased. She could make curtains, rearrange furniture, gather firewood, and not have to ask Marian or any of the Norths if it suited. The freedom she felt was overwhelming and she loved every minute of this new experience.

All of a sudden it dawned on her that she would probably need to find a place to stay in Sudbury or nearby until she could get into the cottage… if she got the cottage. 'Maybe I'm projecting too much," she thought. "Perhaps I should find others to see as well."

Returning back to the Estate Agent section, she was both disappointed and pleased that there were no more available leases listed in Kersey. Turning to the room rental section, she scanned the columns for Sudbury and found several that sounded attractive and decided to discuss them with Mr. Abbott. "He might even have some listings himself," she thought.

Looking at the clock, she decided she'd best start dressing to go to the gallery with Colin. She took a beige linen skirt from the hanger and found a melon colored cotton sweater in her bag. By adding the pearls, it made a nice enough outfit for a Sunday afternoon looking at art. She checked herself in the mirror and noticed that her coloring was a bit pale. "Guess I need some blush, or a bit of sunshine would do," she laughed. "Hope we don't have far to go to the pub. I'm really getting hungry again."

At twelve twenty she started downstairs and was surprised to see Colin on the landing just outside her room. "Hello, Colin. Seems we left our rooms at the same time," she said as she walked toward him.

"Right. Ready for a quick run in the rain?" he asked. "The pub is just around the corner, and the gallery is only a block away. Seems a pity to take the car out of the garage just for a block and some rain. Will you melt?" he laughed. "I have a rather large umbrella, so you shan't get too wet."

Stepping onto the top step, he opened the large silk umbrella and offered her his hand. The rain by now had slowed to a drizzle and she was grateful it was starting to show some patches of blue in the sky.

"Maybe this will clear before soon," she said.

"Don't depend on it, it can rain for days, clear for an hour and start to rain again. Jolly old England!"

They walked to Old Brompton Road, which by now was becoming fairly familiar to her, and crossed over to a pub on the corner, The White Coach. Making their way to a table near the back, he ordered a glass of bitter for both of them. "You'll like it. It is a light ale," he offered as he put his mackintosh on the coat rack.

"Mmm, this is good," she said, but wishing she was eating instead of drinking. "Do you think we can order our lunch? It must be the weather or something, but I am so hungry I could eat the coasters."

"Right. I'll go up to the counter. Would you like a shepherd's pie or maybe some fish and chips."

"The fish and chips sound wonderful. I'll have that, thanks."

Almost embarrassed at the haste in which she was eating, she looked at Colin and said, "Now I know why you all like fish and chips so much. This is delicious and I intend to eat every bit of it."

He laughed. "You must have been really hungry, Patti. Glad I don't have a cat who was depending on your leavings."

Colin paid the bill and they once again stepped out into the mist. It was raining just enough to use the umbrella, and she noticed that he seemed to like holding her arm as they walked. And, she admitted to herself that it was nice to feel a man's touch again. At the next corner they turned back to Onslow Square and walked about four doors down where there was a bright red awning over the doorway of the gallery. They stepped inside and she was impressed with the interior. The walls were painted in varying shades of grey, with white, black and red tables, chairs, and lamps placed among the paintings. Colin led her to the side of the first room, put his arms on her shoulders and turned her to the wall. Gasping, she said, "Oh, my. The Grimshaws." She was visibly thrilled.

"Someday I want to visit Leeds where he lived all his life and see if I can feel a bit of what he felt as he painted these scenes. You know, he was best known for his moonlit scenes, but looking at this one, it looks like daylight to me," she said as she intently studied a painting of a lady with parasol sitting in a garden. It was Grimshaw's

In the Pleasaunce: the garden at Knostrop Hall. Grimshaw had rented the Knostrop mansion in 1870 and lived there until his death in 1893.

"You would probably enjoy a holiday in Leeds. It is in the Yorkshire region and has many old castles. Do you like castles, Patti?" he asked.

"Hmm. Oh yes, excuse me, but I am so thrilled to be here," she said, apologizing for her obvious distraction. "This is a lovely gallery. Do you suppose I could get some brochures from them... for my research, you know."

"Right. I know the owners. Be right back." He left her staring now at a Thomas Girtin print of his *Kirkshall Abbey.* She was in another world and very far from Cleveland at that moment.

Colin came back in a few minutes and handed her a red leatherette folio. Inside were several brochures about the gallery and some flyers of upcoming exhibits. She briefly looked at them, but noticed one that particularly caught her attention. "Colin, I shall have to come back next month. They're having a Winslow Homer exhibit, and I've always been fond of his work."

"How fortunate. May I have the pleasure of being your escort?" he asked with a decided gleam in his eye.

"We'll have to see how my research schedule goes in Kersey and if I really can get away," she answered, not wanting to increase his expectations.

Leaving the gallery they were glad to see that the rain had subsided and the sun was starting to shine. He suggested they stop at the patisserie for a coffee and sweet. She thought this was a good idea and they walked back toward Old Brompton again. After devouring a very large napolean and two cups of espresso, she told him she would like to pick up some books at Waterstone's, which was on the corner of Cranley Place. They went to the bookstore, and as she chose some books on Suffolk, he browsed through the latest collection of Colin Dexter's, *Inspector Morse* series.

"I'm ready to pay for these, Colin. Find anything you like?"

"Yes, think I'll get Dexter's *Last Bus to Woodstock*. Heard it's a good read and somehow I've missed this one."

With purchases in hand, they crossed the street and headed to Number 10. She was beginning to feel like this was *her neighborhood*. Perhaps she could come back to visit occasionally. The company was certainly enjoyable.

The evening meal in the dining room was a fine English fish… plaice… with little boiled potatoes, fresh steamed asparagus and hollandaise and for dessert the chef had made a three-berry torte called "Fruits of the Forest." Finishing with coffee, the meal was delicious and Patti knew there would be nights alone in Kersey when she would wish she were back here partaking of this wonderful fare. Hopefully she would have the funds and opportunity to practice her culinary skills, limited though they were.

She bid good night to the other guests, sent her compliments to the chef via Maureen, and tapped Colin on the shoulder to tell him good bye. He sat at another table tonight and she was somehow glad, but confused, at this choice. He immediately rose and taking her arm, led her to the outer foyer near reception.

"Are you retiring so early?"

"Yes, Colin. I need to pack and make my plans to get to the train station tomorrow morning. Think I leave from Liverpool station, but need to call for departure times. I must be in Sudbury right after lunch," she answered as he stood staring at her.

"Patti, I'll be glad to drive you to the station, if you'd like."

"No, Colin, I'll take a taxi. It will be better."

He took her hand and together they walked out into the cool May night. There on the sidewalk, which was void of people, he put his arms around her shoulders, pulled her to his chest and kissed her gently.

She felt a shiver go up her back and moved away. "Colin, please. I'm not in a position to respond to your actions. You are a most kind man and I could be fond of you, but not today. But, I will take it as a compliment that you have shown me this attention."

Closing the door to her room, she reflected on the events of this very special weekend. "What a marvelous, enlightening, and most confusing start of my adventure," she thought as she started to get her bags out for repacking. "Most enlightening, indeed."

CHAPTER FOURTEEN

TURNING FOR A LAST LOOK…at the Tramore, Patti got into the black taxi and was on her way to Victoria Station where she would take another train and then change to still another at the Liverpool Street Station that would take her to Sudbury. Maureen stood on the stone steps and waved as the taxi pulled away. Colin was not there to say good-bye, and it was just as well, she thought. His friendship filled a special need for her at this time, but she felt it totally unfair to encourage his attentions.

The morning was misty and the click, click of the windshield wipers lulled her into a state of quiet solitude. Not even the heavy morning traffic nor the honking of horns could interrupt her dozing and thinking about the past few days. She felt as though she had been in a dream and this was not really happening. Suddenly, with the screech of the brakes and the loud cursing of the driver, she found herself sliding off the leather seat and almost prone on the floor.

"Sorry, ma'am. Tha' bugger decided to stop without lettin' the rest 'o the world know. Hope you didn't hurt yourself none."

"I'm fine," Patti declared as she sat back on the seat and found her handbag, which had slid under the seat. That woke her up.

Victoria Station was immense and she had to search the huge lighted overhead signs to find her track. All of her bags, by now much heavier with the addition of the books from Waterstone's, were safely on a cart and she pushed it toward track twelve. The sign was flashing departure at ten fifteen, giving her another thirty minutes before they left. Finding a coffee counter, she ordered a tea and toast and looked around for a seat at one of the small white tables. Spotting a vacant chair, she wheeled the cart over, trying to balance the tea and toast. She realized the man sitting at the other chair at the table had a familiar face. He was a priest, she did not know of what faith, and was wearing his clerical collar and a tweed sport coat. Interesting, she thought.

"Do you mind if I share your table," she asked.

"Please be havin' a seat, ma'am. Looks like you have a load there," he answered as he stood up to pull out her chair.

"Please don't think me forward, but I seem to think we've met before. Of course, that's probably impossible since I'm from the States," she said as she took a sip of the hot tea.

"Well, I used to travel a bit, but haven't been on the road much since I last went to Dublin about three years ago.

"That's where I met you. We were in a park in Dublin... St. Stephen's Green... and we were watching a group of children at play," she said with an excitement in her voice. "You told me you were from Kersey and after you left I remembered that a friend of mine had told me about that village, too."

"Why, bless Pat. You are so right. And what brings you here to England?" he asked.

"I'm, I'm, uh, doing some art research and wanted to visit in the Suffolk region," she answered. Not really wanting to lie, she did intend to enjoy seeking out works of artists from that area.

Looking at his watch, he said, "I must get to track twelve. May I help you to your track? You do have a lot to load on the train. Oh, by the way, my name is Tom Beacham... well, Father Nigel Thomas Beacham. And who are you, may I ask?"

"I'm Patti North, Father, and yes, I'd appreciate your help. I'm also going to track twelve. Uh, you see, I'm going to be staying in Kersey for about six months," she replied as they made their way across the vast terminal shop area and down to the departure tracks.

"You're going to Kersey, too. Wonderful, do hope you'll come to services at St. Mary's. That's where I work."

Tom helped Patti up the steps of the Brit Rail train car and began to load her bags into the storage area, which was in the front of each car.

"Would you care for a seatmate for the journey?" he asked, sitting down before she could respond.

"Why yes, that would be fine." She settled herself at the window seat, he sat opposite her. Each set of seats was divided by a table, which served for writing, eating, or even a place to put a tired head. She looked out the window as the train pulled out of the station and watched as they passed the train yards with stacks of pallets, lined up carts, spare wheels, and other equipment that kept this immense industry on the move.

"Do hope I'm not being too curious, but I was wondering why you're choosing Kersey for your visit," he said as he looked at her, noticing again the wedding set on her left hand. He had remembered that from three years ago.

She looked away from the window, and clearing her throat, said, "I guess I should be honest, especially to a priest, but in the simplest of words, I've run away from home... just like a bad, little girl."

"Oh, you don't look like a bad, little girl to me. There must be some very important reason for you to leave home and come here by yourself," he said reassuringly, all the while taking in the essence of her beauty... the silky blond hair, the clear blue eyes, and the tall, graceful body that complemented her obviously expensive clothes.

His maleness, despite some inhibitions from his profession, was stirring and he rather liked the feeling.

Her emotions would not stay down. She started to cry and was trying to find a handkerchief from her pocket, when he reached over, took her hand and said. "Now, Mrs. North. Don't get upset. You needn't tell me anymore."

"That's okay, I need to talk to someone. Perhaps confession to a priest would help. And, please call me Patti."

"I'm not a Catholic priest," he said, "but we Anglicans do accept confession on occasion... Patti."

"Oh," she sighed. "At home we're Episcopalian. Isn't that close to Anglican?"

"Yes, we're the Mother Church, so to say. But you don't report to our Archbishop," he answered with a laugh. She liked the way his soft brown eyes sparkled when he laughed. Studying him further, she silently admired his thick dark, blond hair which almost touched that white collar. He seemed to be about six feet two or three, although she wasn't good at judging men's height, and did not wear a wedding band. That bringing a sense of guilt, she looked away and stared out the window.

Again he tried to make conversation. "Do you have transportation to Kersey once you arrive in Sudbury?"

"Yes, an Estate Agent is picking me up and taking me to see a cottage that's for lease. I'll find a room in Sudbury for a few days, or until I find a place to lease that's ready for occupancy." She didn't feel it was necessary to tell him much more, even if he was a priest. It was almost like someone reading your diary and discovering your secrets. This was to be her own special adventure and she was not ready to share it... with anyone.

As the conductor announced arrival at Liverpool Street Station, Tom again offered to help her, and though she really didn't want to have further obligation, she felt tired and accepted his offer.

The next leg of the journey would include nineteen possible stops before they reached Marks Tey, where they would get off and board still another train... a two-car open-window train to go the last twelve miles.

Passing little villages with strange names... Ilford, Gidea Park, Hatfield Peverel, Tiptree... they both were quiet, Tom feeling her need for privacy. She appreciated his perceptiveness and guessed it was part of the role of a priest.

"Marks Tey, all off to change to Chappel & Wakes Colne, Bures and Sudbury," came the conductor's loud announcement. Again they gathered up their belongings and got off the train.

Inside the two room station at Marks Tey, they were told the train was being serviced down the track and would be about twenty minutes late. Patti was starting to get very hungry and felt a bit squeamish. Looking around the station, she noted that there was no food or drink to be had, save for a water fountain. The tea and toast had long since left and she longed for a sandwich and a soda.

"I could sure do with a bit of lunch. Do you think there's any place nearby that we can get a sandwich?" she asked the pimply faced young station agent.

"No ma'am. You'll not be findin' any place to buy a bite until you get to Sudbury," looking up as he stopped counting his tickets.

She remembered some crackers she had stuck in the back of her carry-on bag and vigorously tried to find them. Once found, she offered some to Tom, who declined, and then proceeded to devour all three packs. "Something about soda crackers that always calms the tummy," she laughed as she deposited the empty wrappers in a tall trash barrel.

As they walked outside the station, she realized that she was in *Constable Country* where Thomas Constable painted along the River Stour. Thinking to herself, she promised to come back this way often to discover some of that beauty in person, picturing in her mind his most famous, *The Hay Wain,* and some of his finest of Willy Lott's farm.

Soon they heard the clickety clack of the little two-car train as it pulled into the station. The windows were all open and the conductor moved from the front to the back to drive, depending on which direction they were headed. The passenger seats also reversed to face to Sudbury or Marks Tey. They got on, found a seat at the front of the second car and laughed as it pulled away from the little stone station.

"I am having such a good time," Patti said as she patted Tom's arm, and then realizing what she had done, she quickly withdrew it and gave him a weak smile.

"Glad you are now," he said and then very seriously said," Let me give you my card. Please call me when you get settled in Sudbury. It's always good to have a contact in a strange place and perhaps I can help you with your arrangements in Kersey. We're not a very big village and most of the people are my parishioners."

The train slowly made it's way west to Sudbury, passing fields and patches of trees overhanging the tracks and the River Stour. They also crossed the Chappel viaduct, built in 1849 with 32 brick arches high above the River Colne. Next came the East Anglian Railway Museum. They passed Bures, and finally the end of the line, Sudbury.

Tom again helped Patti with her bags, setting them down on the sidewalk outside the station. She had told him she needed to call the Estate Agent when she arrived, so he said he would wait by her bags, holding his umbrella over them from the noon day mist. She called Mr. Abbott and he said he would be there in ten minutes.

"Just look for a little green car, that'll be me."

Patti thanked Tom and told him she would call when she got settled. He smiled, and with internal protest, refrained from expressing anything more than cordiality. Hoping their paths would cross, and knowing for sure in a such a small village they would, he held out his hand and bid good-bye. She watched as he walked to the parking lot, observing his long-gaited stride as he approached a small black sedan. Tom waved back to her as he circled out of the drive and made a right turn toward Kersey.

The sound of a squeaky horn came from Mr. Abbott's car and he stopped right in front of Patti. Since she was the only person waiting on the sidewalk, he didn't have to wonder if it was she. "Hello, there. You must be Mrs. North," he called out as he slammed the car door.

"Yes, and you are Mr. Abbott?" she asked.

"Right. Let me get your bags in the car and we'll be on our way." Tall, lanky, and a bit hunched over, Charles Abbott nevertheless had the quick step of a younger man. He placed the bags into the car trunk with ease, then held the door for Patti to enter.

As they left the station Charles Abbott drove through the center of Sudbury and gave her a little history of the town, noting that it was the home of the painter, Thomas Gainsborough, and thought she might like to visit his home and gardens some day. She looked with delight at all the shops with their various wares, and saw a small department store that she hoped would have the things she'd be needing to set up housekeeping. It was directly across from the old stone church, now a city building. She also saw a taxi waiting for a fare and guessed she'd be one of his regular customers since there was no public transportation to Kersey and she certainly didn't plan to buy a car.

They drove out the A1071, through Boxford, and at Hadleigh turned north. Nearing Kersey she could see the top of St. Mary's Church and surmised this was Tom's church. It was on top of one of the two hills surrounding Kersey and made a very imposing picture as they approached the village.

"What is the name of the main street in Kersey?" she asked Charles Abbott.

"The Street," he answered.

"No, the *name* of the street."

"That is the name, The Street," he laughed.

Turning the corner onto the road with no curbs or sidewalks, they passed the old wooden pump on the right, somewhat symbolic with Kersey, and then all of a sudden in front of her she saw it... Kersey, "running steeply down The Street to a water-splash through a tributary of the Brett, and up again, just as steeply, to the summit of Church Hill" (as described in the Book of British Villages). She sighed and silently said a prayer that she had made it this far.

Called a "toy town" by some, the village's red-tiled roofs and houses painted in hues of red, ochre, beige, white and pink, somehow disguised the actual age of the community. A wall by the river, when shed of it's summer growth, showed a date-mark of 1490. The River House was said to be inhabited for over 500 years, and the residents had the sweet lulling sound of the water and the occasional quack of the ducks for company. The black boards of the timbered houses were said to have been tarred for preservation.

Patti saw the old weaver's cottages where almost all of England's Kersey cloth was made in years' past and from whence came most of the money to build magnificent churches and cathedrals. She was delighted to see that many of the houses had window boxes or pots on the steps with gaily-colored flowers. They passed the old Bell Pub and the Kersey Pottery, crossed the swail and saw the ducks preening themselves. Turning right at the next lane, Brett Lane, Charles Abbott drove to the end and turned left next to a salmon colored house with a thatched roof. Continuing down the long driveway, they pulled into a turnaround beside a small, white, stone cottage that had shutters of a dark brown, almost black.

"This is it," he announced, slamming the car door. She got out, and stood looking in amazement for a few moments. The growth of weeds and untrimmed shrubs nearly covered the front door and the small porch. "That will be a good weeks' work," she thought as she watched Charles Abbott struggle with the key. After a few twists and a hefty shove with his shoulder, the door opened. He went in ahead of her and turned on an overhead light from a switch behind the door. From the glaring naked bulb, she could see immediately what he meant about some clean-up being required. It was obvious that the cottage had been vacant for some time and you could definitely detect that it needed a "woman's touch" with a sturdy broom and a large scrub bucket.

As they walked into the room, she saw a folding gate-leg dining table and four sturdy chairs, all needing a good coat of polish. The living area had a small, lumpy, overstuffed sofa that was covered in a flowered print of various colors. A rather tiny side chair sat beneath the window and in front of the sofa was a battered coffee table. "I can refinish that," she mused. Also facing the sofa was a stone fireplace that showed obvious marks of past use. Behind the living area and next to the dining space, was a kitchenette with a fair sized sink, small stove with three burners and an oven, and a refrigerator that meant frequent marketing, due to it's size. At the right of the entrance was a door into the bedroom, which was only large enough for the full size bed (or was it three-quarters?), an armoire, a small nightstand and a petite, dark wood chair. Gingerly easing over to the bathroom door, she gave a sigh of relief to see a nice sink, commode and a wonderful, deep bathtub for those luxurious soakey baths. From the uneven woodworking on the walls and ceilings, it was apparent that this room had been added long after the cottage was built.

"Well, what 'ya be thinkin'? Will it do for your needs, miss?" he asked as she stood quietly contemplating all the work it would take to be clean again.

"Mr. Abbott, if I can find someone to help me do some small repairs and paint, I think it will be most satisfactory. And, yes, I want to take it. Oh yes, tell me about the owners."

"Right. Harriet and Richard Olmsted. They aren't around much, they aren't. Both work in London and only come out here on weekends. Sometimes she comes 'round for a week or two in the summer. Usually brings her nephews with her to help with the yard. Other times I send someone over to tidy up."

"Do you thing they will mind if I do some repairs and improvements?" she asked, hoping for a positive reply.

"I'd be supposin' they'd be most grateful to find someone willin' to do just that."

As they were getting back into his little green car, she turned and asked him if it would be possible to drive up to the church. He said that was not a problem and headed back up The Street to the top of Church Hill, telling her that St. Mary's was built in the 14th century and also housed a school for the village children. She could see the paths among the tall grasses where they obviously walked on their way to and from home. Tucking this information in the back of her mind, she briefly gave thought to applying for a job teaching art to the children. After all, "I'm going to need to find some way to make money. My little stash won't last too long." The stone church with it's walls of square-split flint and stone, had beautifully preserved carved panels on the south porch… "Masterpieces from the 15th century," he continued to tell her. Since it had suffered mass destruction during the Reformation, there were several headless angels among the other artifacts, but he said each generation of parishioners had offered their part in preserving some of the treasures, like a 15th century screen of kings and prophets making double-jointed gestures with their hands, the church bells, and some embroidered ecclesiastical hassocks. Patti was totally enchanted with this information and hoped she would learn more, possibly someday from Father Beacham... Tom.

They drove back down The Street and toward Sudbury. It was starting to get dark and Patti was suddenly concerned about where she would stay for the night.

"Mr. Abbott, did you say you might have some listings of rooms where I could stay for a few days until the cottage is ready?"

"Oh yes. Now don't you be a worryin'. My wife said she'd be glad to have you stay with us for a few days. I didn't be sayin' anythin' about it until I checked you out. You seem like a nice lady. We didn't want to be offerin' lodgin' to just anyone you see."

"Well, I certainly want to pay you. Please let me know what you need and I can pay in advance for, say, four nights."

"That's all right. We can talk about it later. You're probably tired and could do with a nice dinner and a rest. Looks like you got a lot 'o cleanin' ahead o' you," he laughed as he parked the car on the curb in front of a plaster sided house about two blocks from the town center.

He helped her in with her bags, she met Priscilla Abbott, and was shown to a little bedroom decorated in pink rose wallpaper, pink rose curtains, rose printed bedspread, and a rose flowered rug on the clean, polished floors. She could almost smell the roses.

After a most ample dinner of roast chicken, noodles, fresh brussel sprouts, and an apple cobbler, she excused herself and took a nice hot bath. Before closing her eyes, Patti thought about the day's events, seeing Father Beacham again, making the commitment for the cottage and accepting the Abbotts hospitality. "My apprehensions and fears are turning into acceptance and contentment over this drastic change I've made in my life. If only the future will stay calm so that I might realize peace." Sleep came swiftly and she was grateful for nice people and a cozy warm bed.

CHAPTER FIFTEEN

RAYS OF SUNLIGHT... beamed into her *rose* room and she stretched and yawned like a cat awakening from an afternoon nap. The smell of bacon and eggs was in the air and for a moment she had the feeling she was back home at the Meads. Putting on her purple silk robe and slippers, she went out into the kitchen.

"Good morning, Mr. and Mrs. Abbott. That sure smells good."

"And a good mornin' to ya', too. Hope you got a big appetite. My wife likes to cook for an army, she does," Charles Abbott remarked with pride as he poured a cup of tea for Patti.

"Do hope you slept well," Priscilla Abbott commented as she heaped the bacon and eggs on each plate.

"Oh yes, the bed was very comfortable and I don't think I stirred until just a few minutes ago." She added some much needed salt to the eggs and decided to pass on the toast. "I must cut back on my eating. Seems all I've done since I left Cleveland is eat, eat, eat."

"Did you say Cleveland?" asked Priscilla. "My cousin lives there in an apartment near the lake. She keeps askin' us to come for a holiday, but Charles' work never gives him a day to hisself. Maybe you know her, her name is Heather Summerfield and she works at a place called Higbees."

"Well, I certainly know Higbees, spent an awful lot of my money in that store, but don't think I know your cousin. Cleveland is one of our largest cities."

Finishing her breakfast, Patti told Charles that she was going to walk into town after she dressed and wanted to try and find a handyman to help her fix up the cottage. He gave her the name of a man in the next block who did odd jobs and "seems a nice enough bloke." His name was John Dunthorne, a man about fifty, who had lost his job at the cloth factory some years ago and started doing odd work for the townspeople. "Word around here has it that he had a small problem with the pints and couldn't keep his hours at work," Charles stated hesitatingly, not wanting to frighten her. "But I never seen evidence o' his bein' tipsy." She felt she would at least meet the man and draw her own conclusions.

The day was beautiful, clouds high in the sky and a slight breeze blowing. She enjoyed slowly walking down the street from the Abbott's house and found her way to the department store she had seen yesterday. Nailed to the side of the front entrance was a sign painted in yellow and blue... *WINCH & BLOTCH* . The front windows were full from corner to corner with samples of the wares inside. White lace curtains draped one side of the west window, framing stacks of flowered dishware, striped towels, bright multi-colored bedspreads, and boxes of assorted kitchen utensils. The east window was an array of luggage, books, shoes, and gaily patterned ladies dresses. Men's shirts with striped ties hung in behind them, offering a somber backdrop to the dresses. Stepping inside she knew this would be where she would do most of her serious shopping. Two salesladies, who said they were best friends, but one liked Maggie Fletcher, the other didn't, waited on her with anxious courtesy and offered their suggestions for her purchases. By the time she left the store one hour later, the *helpful* ladies had *helped* her spend three hundred dollars in bed linens, towels, cookware, dishes and flatware, two brooms, a mop, and a few items they said she just must have… like a large bottle of bubble bath. That she did need. They assured her it would all be delivered late today to the cottage and asked her to invite them to tea soon… friendly sorts.

On the way back to the Abbotts she found John Dunthorne's house and rang the bell. The door opened, and facing her was a huge man with bushy red hair and a big smile on his face. "Hullo," said the big man as he stepped out to the sidewalk. "What can I do fer 'ya?"

"Mr. Abbott said you might be available to do some repair work and painting at a cottage he's just leased to me."

"Might."

"Well, I need someone to start right away, tomorrow morning, in fact," she said, awaiting his answer.

"How much ya' be payin'?"

"I can offer you £20 a day. Does that seem fair? And no drinking on the job," she hastily added.

"I don't drink at me work, ma'am. I'm a hard worker, I am."

"Well," she impatiently asked, "Can you work for me, or not?"

"Right. Well, 'spose I can start tomorrow. But I have to have Saturday off. Me friend's ridin' a horse at the race and I got a bet on 'im. He's a fast horse, he is."

"Fine. You'll have to find your way there, it's in Kersey, at the Olmsted house on Brett Lane. I'm leasing the cottage in back. I don't have a car and will have to take a taxi myself."

He gave her a big smile. "Right. I can get a ride with me friend. He passes that way to the stables. I'll be out there about eight-tomorrow morning. That be okay?"

"Yes, fine. I'll see you tomorrow morning, Mr. Dunthorne."

Feeling more confident now that her plans were finally coming together, she stopped in a tea room across from Gainsborough's house and had a scone and hot herb tea. She wished she had time to tour the house and gardens, but that would have to wait for another day. She wanted to get back to the Abbotts and make some entries in her notebook. She planned to list each room, that wouldn't take long considering the size of the cottage, and then list all the things she had to do in each room. Starting at the front door, she knew the first thing to be done tomorrow morning was cutting back all the overgrowth. "A good scrub on the front steps wouldn't hurt either," she decided, and that brought her to remembering that the windows were so dirty they looked like frosted glass. "They will surely need a good cleaning with vinegar and water." Suddenly she remembered that she needed cleaning supplies and some sort of snacks for lunches. Walking back to the Abbott's street, she found a small grocery store and went in. It took no time at all for her to load a small cart with vinegar, soap powder, cleanser, hand soap, bleach, paper towels, toilet paper, and cheese and crackers for lunch. This filled two big bags and she could hardly lift them, feeling very weak all of a sudden. She stopped and leaned on the checkout counter for a minute to catch her breath and then started out the door.

The Abbotts were glad to know she had found John Dunthorne and offered to take her to the cottage tomorrow so she wouldn't have to juggle all the supplies by herself. She gladly accepted their offer and promised herself that she would do something very special for them in the days to come.

Patti could hardly sleep that night, filled with anxiety about working on her *own little nest.* Over and over she mentally walked through each room and imagined how it would look when she finished. She tried to decide what type of curtains to put at the window and thought she best wait until the cleaning was complete. It was hard to imagine new crisp curtains on windows in what was now a shabby atmosphere.

Wednesday morning finally arrived and she bounded out of bed, humming a tune from *Cats.* "That's an idea. I'll get a cat when I move in." Even though she would have preferred a dog, it seemed to her that a cat would be less trouble and she wouldn't have as much trouble finding a home for it when she left. *When she left...* how she hated to even think of that now. "Who knows, maybe I'll stay forever," she laughed as she put on her jeans and sweatshirt. Finding her old sneakers, which she had packed for some unknown reason and was now glad, she tied them quickly and hurried out to the kitchen. Priscilla had steaming bowls of oatmeal waiting and it took Patti no time at all to finish one and ask for another. "Where am I getting this appetite?" she asked herself.

The drive to the cottage seemed to take hours, when in reality it was only twenty minutes. She loved watching the fields with the flocks of birds flying in and out of the growing grain and the roadsides abundant with wild flowers. She knew she would have to plant flowers as soon as possible. Charles and Priscilla helped her unload the supplies and they all saw the big boxes from the department store at the door. The delivery people had covered them with plastic in case of rain and had assured her they would be safe beside the cottage. They were. Everything she had bought was in the boxes and she was anxious to get started. It was a little after eight, and no John Dunthorne. The Abbotts left, told her not to worry, John would probably be along soon, and told her not to work too hard. "Ha, if he doesn't show I'm going to work really hard."

They were right. About eight thirty he came walking down the gravel driveway, whistling what sounded like an Irish tune. "With that red hair, surely he must be part Irish," she thought as she called to him.

"Good morning, John. Ready for some challenges?" laughing as she grabbed a set of clippers Charles had loaned to her, "Here, you can start at the front by clearing the way so we can at least find the door."

"Right, miss," he answered as he took off his jacket and threw it over a cherry tree limb next to the cottage. He took the clippers and started, continuing to whistle as he worked.

Patti went inside and taking a big bag out of her supply, she started picking up bits of trash… old newspapers, cans of food that had been on the shelves for too long, a houseplant that had died longer ago than she wanted to imagine, dried up cleaning supplies from under the sink, out-of-date medications in the bathroom… and took all this out back to a big trash barrel that had obviously been turned over by some night critters looking for food. Her next chore was to beat the old rugs. The dust that come out of them would have filled the trash barrel, but she kept beating with the broom until she felt she could stand to have them under her feet. She gave the same treatment to the sofa, but swiftly decided a spray disinfectant might be wise and then a new slipcover. The present cover was terribly stained from unknown substances and made her queasy to even think about it.

Patti and John next tackled the window washing and made it into a sort of *assembly line* job, with him taking off the thick layer of dirt and she finishing with wiping them dry. Soon the inside of the house became lighter. She had not realized how much light all that dirt kept out. As they worked together, he told her about his family. He had come to Sudbury from Bantry, County Cork, in Ireland with his wife and six children, hoping to find a better life. He had a good job with the cloth company in their accounting department, but with the introduction of so much technology, the company cut their staff by a third and he lost his job. His wife did day work for some wealthy people and he did odd jobs. All the children had grown and moved away from Sudbury, most going to London where there were more jobs. He took his lot in life with easy stride and said he was a happy man. And, he said he did like his pints, but never when he worked. She found him to be honest and kind.

Patti didn't confide too much about herself to him, but stuck to the research story. She did share with him about her parents and how she knew loss was not easy, whether it was a job or people. The first day went fast and about five John said he was ready to stop. Patti could have worked for hours more, but knew she had to get back to Sudbury soon. They closed up the cottage, admired the results of their hard work and walked back to The Street. Patti went into the Bell Pub and used their telephone to call for a taxi. She waited out on the side of the street, counting the boards on one of the black and white timbered buildings. She saw the general store across the street and made a mental note to stop in there tomorrow to see what she might find for their lunch. Cheese and crackers was not too exciting. From where she was standing though, it didn't look like they had a very big inventory and probably nothing green and fresh.

Not until she got into bed that night did she realize how tired she was and it took no time at all for her to fall asleep. The next morning,

169

Thursday, she told the Abbotts that she had arranged for the taxi to pick her up at seven forty-five, and the driver was there at exactly the requested time. She also arranged for him to pick her up at the cottage at five that afternoon. The driver was a jolly man from Lavenham, north of Kersey, and told her lots of stories about the people who lived around there. He also said she'd have to visit the air museum with all of the planes from *the big war.* Guess he would see her as a good account, one he could depend on for frequent business. She was glad he was a pleasant man and she felt safe with him.

This day Patti and John scrubbed the floors and the bathroom, cleaned out cabinets and painted the bedroom walls a pale yellow.

Friday Patti knew she would have to get as much done with John as possible since he could not work on Saturday and she wanted very much to move in on Sunday. They finished painting the other rooms and he completed cleaning up the yard, cutting back some small trees, pulling out large vines and digging out weeds from around the foundation. He worked hard and never took breaks except to eat the lunch she offered, which improved with each day, thanks to the general store, which had an acceptable selection of canned meats and fresh baked bread. They put away their tools and Patti paid him his wages. He thanked her, shook her hand and said he hoped his wife could meet her someday soon. She told him she would like that and would stay in touch.

Saturday Patti went back to the department store and the ladies again helped her with her shopping. She bought white lace curtains, definitely English, for all of the windows except the kitchen. Here she had decided she wanted old-fashioned gingham tiebacks like she remembered her mother had had in their kitchen so many years ago. Keeping her colors in yellows and blues, she chose yellow gingham. Finding a blue/beige/white plaid slip cover for the sofa, the ladies then *miraculously* came up with four blue pillows that they said could go on the sofa, or on her new yellow and white bedspread. She agreed and indulged herself in this purchase. She also bought a pretty lace tablecloth and some napkins, for those times the ladies came to tea. Or, someone else.

The Abbotts insisted on helping her move the last of her belongings in to the cottage, refusing also to let her pay for her room. She was overcome with their generosity and before they left she asked them to join her in the first pot of tea in *her* home. They stayed for about an hour and then left, Charles saying he had a card game with his friends that evening.

Alone for the first time in her own home, she walked from corner to corner and felt such a sense of joy and freedom. The clean windows, the fresh paint and the new curtains transformed this neglected little house into a warm and charming home. Peace flooded her soul, but she also felt a bit of nausea and realized she hadn't had anything to eat since breakfast. That mixed with the excitement of the move was surely making her weak and ill, so she went over to her little kitchenette and put on a pot of water to boil some potatoes. There was a knock at the door. It frightened her at first, but looking through the glass on the top of the door, she saw a boy of about ten standing there with a big bouquet of flowers.

"Hello. These are for you."

"Well, thank you. But who sent them?" she asked as he was running down the drive.

"The man on the hill," he hollered as he went out on to the lane.

She shut the door and placed the pretty blossoms on the coffee table.

"Thank you, man on the hill," smiling, with a warm feeling in her heart.

CHAPTER SIXTEEN

STRANGE DREAMS… filled her head as she slept the first night in the cottage. First she saw herself back in her mother's sewing room, then she was at the prom with Perry Kessler, next she was in a scene where Marian was screeching orders at the bridesmaids in the wedding. Waking with a feeling of being tired, she went into the kitchen and put on the teakettle… the new brass one that the ladies said she must have in her new home. As she waited for its whistle, she looked out the clean window next to the fireplace and saw the milk truck going down the lane.

"I must call the dairy and start milk delivery," she thought, wishing she had some right now for her tea.

Sensing a need for some faithful reinforcement, she decided to go to the church on the hill, St. Mary's. It was a short walk to the end of Brett Lane and then a climb at the end of The Street. Taking the black knit dress out of her armoire, she then found the black shoes and knew that her feet would ache by the time she got back because these shoes were not the best for walking. "Guess I'll have to spend some money on a pair of low heeled shoes for church. Those *sensible* lace-ups just won't do."

A bit of makeup and a quick brush to her hair, then a look in the armoire mirror and she was ready for the trek up the hill. Closing the cottage door, she caught a whiff of some blossoms from a vine on the back fence. The day felt good.

Several other people were walking up The Street and she supposed they were also going to services. It was near eleven and she hoped she would not be late. The huge carved wooden doors beneath the tower were open, revealing a stained-glass window interior and old wooden pews. An usher, dressed in a grey suit with a flower in his lapel, gave her a program, bid her good morning and offered his arm. They stopped halfway down and she told him that was fine. As she sat down, she looked around at the other people in this old imposing building and was genuinely happy that she chose to come this morning. "These are my new neighbors."

The organ started to play a familiar tune, *Come Thou Almighty King,* and they all rose to sing. The processional began with a young boy acolyte carrying the cross, followed by the lay readers and finally the rector… Father Nigel Thomas Beacham. His head was bowed in obvious prayer as he climbed the steps and sat beside the pulpit. The music stopped and Father Beacham went to the pulpit and began to read the biblical lesson. He read from John, where Jesus asked him to "Feed my lambs", and based his sermon on caring for others. Several times during his sermon, Patti was aware that he was looking at her. She did not return his eye contact and sincerely tried to concentrate on the sermon.

The service ended with the singing of *Faith of our Fathers,* and as the recessional passed, Tom looked her way and smiled. The congregation filed past Father Beacham, each person offering their comments on his sermon, news of the day, or a special need that would require his attention this week. When Patti got to the door and Tom's outstretched hand, she expressed her thoughts of his sermon and turned to go down the steps.

"Mrs. North," he called out, "If you can wait a few minutes, I'd like a few words with you."

"Uh, yes. I'll wait by that oak tree," and she walked over to a knarled old tree that looked as if it had been planted before the church was built.

Tom finished greeting his parishioners and came over to where Patti was patiently waiting.

"Sorry to make you wait, but I wanted to know if you got moved in and how you like our little village."

She returned his big smile and said," I did get all moved in, slept there last night and I think I shall like living in Kersey very much."

There was a feeling of awkwardness in the air and neither of them spoke for a few seconds. Then, at the same time, they both started to make conversation. Tom, bowed and offered his hand in suggestion of her going first.

"Father Beacham, or is it permissible to call you Tom?

"Tom is fine, Patti."

"Well, if you're near Brett Lane one day this week, do stop by and we can share a pot of tea. I'm getting quite good at making it now, not that it takes any great skill, but a new friend, Mrs. Abbott showed me how to steep properly. I feel so competent," she laughed as she realized she was talking like a magpie.

"I'd like to taste your tea, Patti. And I'll bring you some literature on our old church. Do hope you'll be a regular while you're here." Haltingly he added, "And... uh, if I can be of any service in counseling you with your uh, concerns, please let me know. It's my job, you know."

"Very well then, I must get back to the cottage. Still have a lot to do to make it feel like home. Oh, I almost forgot, thank you for the flowers. They're very pretty and you were so nice to send them. It was you, wasn't it?"

With an obvious blush on his face, he said, "You're so very welcome, Patti. Just a show of friendship from the church!" a mischievous smile showing on his face.

She made her way down the hill and on to The Street. Feeling quite happy, she passed Brett Lane and went further down The Street to the Bell Pub. "It's time I start to meet my new business people, too," she thought, as she found a seat near a window.

"Good afternoon, miss. What can we be gettin' ya? A pint?"

"Oh, I'd like a cup of tea and some lunch. What is your special today?" she asked, realizing suddenly how hungry she had become.

"Today the cook has made a good Irish Stew and soda bread."

"That sounds good. I'll have that, thank you," she said as she looked around and noticed she was the only lone female in the pub. There were several couples having lunch or some just enjoying their pints. "Well, I have to eat somewhere and this is where it will be... probably often, too."

The stew had big chunks of lamb and vegetables and a nice thick gravy. The bread was hot and the butter real, not highly processed like in the States. "The cow might even be out back," she mused. Taking the last sip of tea, she put a tip on the table and walked up to the counter to pay her bill.

"You new around here, miss?" asked the chubby man behind the bar.

"Yes, I'm leasing the Olmsted cottage for a few months. I'm Patti North."

"Well, welcome to Kersey. You be needin' anythin', just give us a holler. Me wife and I are here every day… she's Rosie, waited on you just now, and I'm Paddy…Paddy Houlehan."

"Thanks, Paddy. I'll remember your offer." The walk back to the cottage reminded her that she definitely had to buy those low heel shoes… soon.

Patti soaked that night in the tub, having filled it with a generous amount of her newly purchased bath gel, *Boots Sensuous Foaming Bath Esssence with Essential Oils of Llang Llang and Sandlewood.* She enjoyed the warmth and comfort of the hot water as her hair flowed out around her shoulders and she thought about the fact that she needed a hair cut. "Why?" she asked herself. "I am not here to impress anyone. I don't have any social events to attend… it's just me. Heck with the hair cut, I'll tie it back with a ribbon… a yellow one, or a different color for each day," she playfully said out loud. Again the sense of freedom and peace invaded her soul and she felt very good. After putting on her nightgown… with roses… "Wouldn't Priscilla love it?"… she found one of the books on Kersey and started to read. It did not take long for her to reach over, turn off the light, and go to sleep. But before she did, she pondered the feelings she experienced today when she spoke to Tom. She liked talking to him. He was easy to be with… maybe too easy. "I must be careful."

****

WILLIAM DIALED HIS LAWYER… and asking for "Joel Richman, please," he waited for him to pick up the telephone.

"Joel Richman, here," came the abrupt answer from the other end.

"Joel, this is William North…the third. I need to talk to you right away," he said with urgency in his voice.

"Hey, Will, calm down. What's the big problem, somebody steal a painting?" he laughed.

"Hell, no. My wife picked up and left. She's gone to England of all places and I don't know where in England. This is gonna look real bad for the family if it gets out and I need you to get on it now. Norths just don't behave like this." he snapped back.

"Okay, come on down this afternoon at, uh, let's see. Come in at three. And Will, bring anything you think might help. By the way, did she leave a note or anything?"

"Yeah", William said with disgust, "she left a letter telling me she wasn't running away, she was running to. Where the hell 'to' is what I want to know. See you at three. And thanks, Joel"

Thanks were nice, but Joel Richman knew THE Mr. North could pay.

At the stroke of three William entered the offices of Richman, Richman and Seigel in one of Cleveland's pricey new office buildings. Their suite of offices took up the entire twenty-second floor and was lavishly decorated with antiques and several expensive paintings from the North Gallery. He looked down at the receptionist who was busy filing her broken nail, and clearing his throat, announced his arrival.

"I'm here to see Joel Richman."

"What's your name, sir?" she asked in a squeaky voice as she put down the emery board.

"Tell him William North is here… the third."

"Oh, yes sir. I saw your picture in the *Plain Dealer* last week. You won a golf tournament, didn't you?"

"Yeah, that's right. Just tell Joel I'm waiting." With that he sat in a burgundy leather chair and picked up a magazine issued to platinum cardholders of a major credit card organization.

The girl thought to herself how rude and abrupt he was…"Guess you can be that way when you have a lot of money."

"Will, come on in," Joel said as he reached out to shake William's hand. "My office is down this hallway," he added as he led the way

180

past offices of administrative assistants, accountants, mail clerks and other staff necessary to run a law practice of this size. "My assistant would have come out to get you, but she took the afternoon off to go to the doctor."

"No problem, Joel, just glad you could see me today," William answered, glancing into each office.

Joel Richman's office was tastefully done in dark green, navy and cream. His desk was an antique partner's desk and was nearly void of papers and clutter. A corner office, it offered a view of the lake and was the choice location in the suite. He motioned to William to take a seat on the sofa and seated himself opposite in a wingback chair.

Taking his pen out of his pocket, he started to make some notes on a yellow legal pad. "Now William, start from the beginning... from the time you discovered she was gone... and give me all the details."

"On the sixth, this past Thursday, she was supposed to be going up to the cabin at Geneva-on-the-Lake. Mom thought she needed a rest and she also wanted her to do some measuring for drapes or something. I'd been out pretty late the night before with some friends and slept in... had a bit of a hangover, I guess. Mom saw her leave and thought she was going to the cabin. Apparently she drove to her foster parents' house, left the car there and took a taxi to the airport," his voice was cracking a little and he reached into his pocket for his handkerchief.

"I saw an envelope on the bed before I turned in, but put it in a chair and went on to sleep. Didn't get up until about eleven and I was running late for a meeting with a customer and then a golf game, so I didn't read the letter that morning either. After the game my golf partner and I had dinner and went into town to a strip joint... uh, that's another story. Had a little trouble there," stuttering and stumbling on his words a bit.

Continuing, as Joel kept taking his notes, William went on. "I wasn't out too late and Mom and Dad were still up when I got home, so I had a drink with them. Mom said she hadn't been able to reach Patti at the cabin all day... something about those drapes... so I told her I'd try when I went upstairs." He stopped, wiped his nose and his eyes, and with anguish in his voice, said, "As I entered our apartment, for some reason I remembered the envelope and decided to look at it before I called her. Knew it was probably from her... she always left sweet little notes when she went out of town." He was showing signs of regret for waiting so long to look at the envelope. Then, with a sudden change in his remorseful attitude, he exploded as he described the contents of the note. "That ungrateful little bitch, how could she do this to me, to us, the North's… she can't just walk out on me like this."

"Calm down, Will. Let's talk this out rationally and see if we can find her and come to some resolution," Joel said as he evaluated the transposition of his emotions. "I'm going to ask you some questions which you might be uncomfortable answering, but it's necessary for me in order to proceed. First, let me get you a soda or a cup of coffee. What would you like?"

"Just a coke will be fine, thanks,' he answered, a bit more composed.

One of the myriad of staff people, a short, dark haired girl of about twenty-two or three came in with two cokes on a silver tray. Noticing her shapely legs and the tightness of her knit dress, William watched as she seductively walked out of the room smiling to him as she closed the door.

"Alright, let's get down some more facts. First, do you know exactly when she left and on what airline?"

"No."

"Do you know what travel agency she used?"

"No."

"Have you called your regular travel agent for help?"

"No."

"Did you call any of the airlines?"

"No."

"Have you called the police?"

"Absolutely not."

"Will, what HAVE you done," Joel emphatically asked.

"Well, nothing, damn it. My folks told me to get a good night's rest and then tackle it, and then I thought it would just be better to wait until today and talk to you... you're my lawyer, damn it. You're supposed to help me."

"Okay. Let me make some calls. But first, I need a full description of Patti... your description, not mine...her birthday, height, weight, social security number, passport number... those kinds of things. Also, a picture would help if I need it for investigators. Get those things to me as soon as possible, by tomorrow afternoon, please. Also, get me the names and telephone numbers of her closest friends... and those foster parents, too. Have you got it?"

"Yeah, sorry I got angry, but this is a mess. Maybe she had good reason for leaving, I don't know," he admitted.

Joel, looking up from his legal pad, raised his thick eyebrows and said," What do you, mean she might have had good reason? Were you two having problems? I need to know this, Will."

"Ah, no more than any other couple, I suppose. She didn't like me spendin' so much time with my friends. I dunno… guess I could have done more with her, but… ah, forget it. Just find her."

"Will, I'll do all I can, but you've got to cooperate and give me all the information I need… understand? People rarely just disappear for no reason. We'll find her." Standing up, he headed toward the door and asked the dark-haired girl to show him to the front entrance. William thanked him and followed the girl.

CHAPTER SEVENTEEN

LEARNING TO LIVE... on her own and in a foreign country was not nearly as frightening as Patti had anticipated and she was adjusting well. The first two weeks in the cottage she stayed busy arranging and rearranging furniture until she felt it was perfect... for her. First the sofa faced the fireplace, then she moved it to face the front door, then she placed it to the left of the door, and finally it went back to face the fireplace. "I'll be wearing out the new slipcovers just moving this thing," she laughed as she straightened up and felt a pain in her back. "Oh, I really should have asked John to come over and help me with that." Not realizing how heavy and clumsy it was, she sat down on the plump cushions and felt the pain again. The thought of a cup of tea seemed reasonable and as she got up to fill the teakettle, a small trickle of blood dropped on the floor. "Now what, have I pulled something with all this straining?"

Rising early the next morning, Patti found more blood on the sheets and decided this was more than a monthly situation. "Come to think of it," she pondered, "I've been so busy the past two weeks that I haven't even kept track of those days. Maybe it is just that time and I've lost count. Oh well," But the pain was still there and she decided it might be a good idea to find a doctor. Thinking she would have to go back in to Sudbury, she made plans to spend the day there tomorrow. It would be nice to pay a call on the Abbotts and, she could stop in to see the ladies at the department store. "Never know what I might need," she laughed out loud. That afternoon she walked down to the pub and called the taxi company, asking them to pick her up at nine the next morning. After a quick fish and chips with Rosie and Paddy..."Paddy and Patti, we're a fine pair," she had remarked to him, she started back up The Street to the cottage. Just before the water-splash she saw the path leading to the Kersey Pottery and decided to take a look. Banked by hanging vines and tree limbs, the stepping-stone walkway led to the side door of the pottery and in to the showroom where examples of their work was on display. There were jugs, pitchers, mustard pots, plates and candleholders, all in a grey glazed finish with blue designs. She found some candle sticks for her table and a little mustard pot that she determined could also serve as a sugar bowl.

The master potter, Robert Barrows, waited on her and told her how the pottery was made. "The clay is dug from nearby and our potters *throw* the pottery in the back room," where he proceeded to take her. She saw three men and a lady sitting at potter's wheels *throwing* the clay into various shapes. The entire process fascinated her and she followed Mr. Barrows around as he introduced her to each potter and described what they were making.

"Thank you, Mr. Barrows. I really appreciate you taking time to share all this with me."

"Right. We're a small pottery, we are, but we ship a lot to other parts of the continent... some to the States, too," he proudly stated.

"I'm here for about six months, and if you happen to need any help with shipping, or in the showroom, I'd be interested in working for you," she said as she started toward the door. "I'm leasing the Olmsted cottage right across the way on Brett Lane."

"Just might do that, miss. What did you say your name was?"

"Oh, I'm Patti North. Thanks again, Mr. Barrows."

A horn honked just as she was about to cross over the water-splash and the ducks all scattered. Looking up she saw Tom waving at her from his little black car. "Good afternoon, Patti. Can I give you a lift to the cottage?"

"It's just around the corner, Tom. I can walk, but thank you just the same."

He stopped the car and opened the door on her side. "Please, I'd like to talk to you for a bit. That is, if you have a few minutes."

"Well, I guess so. After all, I did invite you to share a pot of tea and today can be the day." She got in and they turned down Brett

Lane. Excitedly she told him about her visit to the pottery and showed him her purchases. "I really enjoyed watching those people make the pottery... absolutely fascinating. Even asked for a job," she laughed as they got out of the car.

Being a pretty day, and since he felt it might look better should anyone drive by, he suggested they bring two chairs out under the trees and have their tea there. She thought that was a bit strange, but went along with his idea. Fortunately she had bought some biscuits... cookies in the states... and added them to the tea tray.

After a cup of tea and some insignificant conversation about the weather he gave her a serious look and said, "Patti, I was wondering if you might be interested in helping at the school. We have a lady who teaches art a couple of times a week, but she has to go in hospital for an operation next week. It would not be too involved, probably following her teaching plans for the year anyway. What do you say?"

Surprised at the offer, she said, "Tom, this is interesting and most coincidental. I've been trying to think of something I could do to add to my income and now two possibilities in one day. Wow, my lucky day."

"Well, do you think you might like to work for say, two days a week from noon to four each day? You would have three classes of children, grades one through six. We double up classes for art."

"That sounds wonderful. How many children are in each class?" she asked, as this started to sound more and more like the answer she was seeking.

"There are about twenty in each of three classes and they don't get real involved in complicated projects. I thought with your art background you might be able to teach them some art history as well as the practical side of making things."

Sensing a need, rather than an obligation to this offer, she responded, "Tom, I'd love to help at the church. Teaching children has always been a desire of mine and it never really found a place in my life. Thank you for this chance to follow a dream."

He reached over and took her hand. Bringing it to his cheek, he looked longingly at her and then abruptly dropped it back into her lap. "I'm sorry, Patti."

"Tom, for what are you sorry? I took that as a gesture of gratitude that I can be of help," she asked, full well knowing that it was much more than that by the look in his eyes.

He stood up and started to bring the chairs back into the cottage. She carried the tea tray and followed him up the steps. The chairs were back in their respective places and the tea tray on the sink counter. Tom came up behind Patti, put his hands on her shoulders, and turning her toward him, stared into her eyes.

"Patti, I make no excuses for the fact that I am very attracted to you. Don't let the collar fool you. Underneath this clerical attire lives a man who appreciates beauty and sincerity. God forgive me, you are a married woman and I have no right to be thinking these things, but I cannot help myself right now. Ever since that day I saw you on the park bench in St. Stephen's Green, you have been haunting my soul."

Gasping, and taking a deep breath, she pulled away from him. "Tom, this… this can't be. Not now. You don't know all about me and it's too complicated for me to even try to explain. Please give me some space, let me get my life sorted out. But, I do want to take the job at the school, if you think it will not confuse things."

Tom looked down at the ground with a hurt look on his face, like a little boy who had just been chastised.

"Sorry. I rarely let my emotions get the best of me, but the moment presented itself and I reacted," he replied as he started toward his car. "Yes, please do take the job and come around tomorrow morning if you can to fill out some papers. Good-bye, Patti. So sorry to have intruded in your life this way. It won't happen again." He backed down the driveway and on to Brett Lane.

"Tom, Tom," she called out as he turned out of the drive, but he was too far to hear her. She had suddenly remembered that she would be going to Sudbury tomorrow to see a doctor. "Guess I'd better call him to change the day." Feelings of caution and ecstasy were fighting within her and she started to cry in anguish. "It's not fair. What I wanted, I got and didn't like. What I like now I can't have." *Be careful what you pray for, you might get it.*

"Father Beacham, please," Patti said as the church receptionist answered her call.

"Father Beacham, here."

"Tom, this is Patti. I tried to catch you as you drove out, but you were too far down the drive to hear me. I will have to change my appointment with you. I, uh, have to go in to Sudbury on business tomorrow morning."

"Oh, that's fine, Patti. Just let me know when you'd like to be comin' round. Thanks for calling... and thanks for the tea."

The taxi driver knocked on the door at five 'til nine the next morning and she called out for him to wait a minute. She grabbed her umbrella and coat, as it looked like rain for sure today.

"Mornin', miss. Ready to go in to Sudbury?"

"Thank you. I want to stop at the Abbotts house first, and then could you wait for a few minutes? Have to get an address from them."

Clouds hung low over the fields and the driver turned the wipers on on the *windscreen.* It had started to rain as they rounded the corner at the end of The Street and turned on to the A1071. Patti closed her eyes and tried to count days so she could be accurate with the doctor. Somewhere in the back of her mind she had memories of an event that could be the reason for this curious happening in her life.

The little taxi motor purred as Patti jumped out and ran up to the Abbott's door. A heavy knock and a quick look inside the front window showed her that they were just finishing breakfast. Priscilla opened the door. "Patti, how nice to see you, darlin'. Come in."

"Priscilla, I just need to talk to you for a minute. Can we sit in the parlor?"

"Sure, darlin'. Let me tell Charles you've come 'round."

"No, can we just talk alone first, please," she pleaded.

"Oh, 'spose that'd be fine."

All things do not work as planned. Charles came into the room and gave her a big hug. "Patti, darlin'. What 'ya be doin' in town so early in the mornin'?"

"Oh, I have some shopping to do and wanted to ask Priscilla some questions."

Winking at Charles, Priscilla went over and took his arm. "You be cleanin' up the dishes, Charles, and let me have some time with Patti." He dutifully obeyed and went back into the kitchen.

"Priscilla, I've been having some bleeding and some pain in my stomach the past few days and think I really should see a doctor. Do you know of one who might see me on short notice like this?"

"Oh, Patti, darlin'. I hope this isn't serious. Yes, Doctor Tolbert down the way would probably see 'ya. He's been takin' care of our family for years and has a nice young doctor from Wales who just joined 'im. Do you want me to call 'im for 'ya?"

"Well, I've asked the taxi driver to wait. Had thought I'd just take my chances and show up. Don't mind waiting. Anyway, I want to stay in town today and do some shopping. Just let me have his address and I'll be on my way."

Priscilla went over to the desk and wrote down the address. Handing Patti the note, she hugged her and said, "Patti, if 'ya be needin' some motherin', please call me." Patti kissed her on the cheek, called out to Charles and went out to the taxi.

Doctors Alan Tolbert and Andrew Burton, General Practitioners, had offices on Blake Street, west of the center of Sudbury. Housed in an old two-story stone building that had been a rooming house, the doctors made use of the entire space. The first floor was reception and here sat a lady with grey hair pulled back in a knot. The walls were lined with chairs of several styles, offering varying degrees of comfort. The second floor was examining and minor surgery rooms, and the third floor was offices and a well-fitted medical library.

Patti closed the door behind her and gave the receptionist her name.

"Do you be havin' an appointment, miss?"

"No, I'm new in this country and Mrs. Abbott suggested I come in to see the doctor," Patti answered.

"Which doctor do you want to be seein.?"

"I guess it doesn't matter. I just need to talk to one of them about my problem."

"Well, they're both at hospital doin' an operation this mornin'. Could 'ya find your way to do some shopping or have a coffee and then come back in about two hours?" Pulling her glasses down to the end of her nose, she gave Patti a studious once over.

"Yes, that would be fine. I'll do that and come back at one. Is that okay?" she asked disappointedly.

"Right. We'll see 'ya back here after lunch."

Patti walked back about four blocks to the center of town and made her way to a *Boots* pharmacy. She was in desperate need of toothpaste and wanted to find some more of that wonderful bath gel. It was purple, came in a bottle with a twist topper and made the longest lasting bubbles she could remember. With a little prayer for the nice deep tub at the cottage, she walked up and down the aisles familiarizing herself with the differences in names and packaging. Even something as simple as a bar of soap looked so attractive here. "Perhaps," she thought, "we just take too much for granted in the States." She found the bath gel and the toothpaste and added them to some other items she had put in the wire basket, then headed to the check-out.

Out on the sidewalk she turned left and went into the department store. *The ladies* were at a counter in the back of the store. She waved to them and they came out from behind the counters and greeted her with open arms. "Hello, Mrs. North. So nice 'ta see 'ya back in Sudbury. What can we be doin' for 'ya today?" they said in unison.

"You know, it's about time I learned your names, too." Patti said as she gave them each a hug.

Giggling like school girls, they responded. "I'm Cynthia Stiles," said the shorter of the two. She had graying hair, which was cut just below her chin. Wearing a print dress and sensible shoes, she could have been anyone's mom or school teacher.

"And, my name's Margaret Overstreet," said the taller one with short blond hair. Appearing to be in their late forties, they said they had been childhood friends and both worked at the department store since they had finished school. Margaret wore a beige polyester blouse and black skirt that was well below her knees. She too had the sensible shoes. "Guess all the English wear them," Patti thought to herself.

Patti told the two friends that she was looking for some low-heeled shoes… walking up that hill from The Street to the church was going to present a challenge. They took her over to the shoe department, apparently they worked all areas of the store, and started to take some boxes off the wall shelves. She chose a pair of very plain, black pumps with the *sensible* heel and a pair of beige, cloth shoes that she could use in the house or in the garden she wanted to plant. Passing the kitchen department, Patti noticed some pretty tea cups and saucers with flowers and gold trim. The ones she was using now matched her plain dishes and she wanted something fancier for tea with friends. These were added to the shoe purchases and the ladies stacked her things on the counter. Thinking about her new job… or perhaps two new jobs… she realized the few clothes in the armoire would not do. "I certainly can't wear that black knit to teach in and slacks are not appropriate either."

At the ladies dress section she looked through the limited selection. These were not at all what she was used to in Cleveland, of course, but decided not to be picky. The multi-colored prints with flowers, or birds, or feathers did not suit her taste at all. Finding a plain navy jacket and skirt, she tried to find a couple of blouses that would stretch this outfit. Cynthia and Margaret brought four blouses out of the back room.

"These just came in and would look ever so lovely on 'ya," Cynthia said as Margaret held one up to Patti's face.

"Oh, and the color's just right for 'ya, too," chimed in Margaret. So, she chose two of the blouses, one in white and one in pink… no flowers.

Patti gave them her Visa card, thanked them for their help and started out the door. She hesitated a moment and then knew it was too late. "Really shouldn't have put that on the credit card. William will get the bill and know where it came from. Oh well, it will happen sooner or later anyway."

****

The New Paris Tea Room, a few doors from the department store, had a chalk easel outside advertising *Spinach Crepes* and *Kidney Pie* as lunch specials. She knew the kidney pie would not be her choice, but the crepes sounded good and she was indeed hungry. A glass of chardonnay wine complimented the crepes and she finished it all in short order. Looking at her watch she noted that it was close to one and she'd better hurry for her appointment.

Entering the office she saw that reception was full of people. She let the receptionist know she was there and found a seat near the door. Without looking up, the woman handed her a clipboard with forms and asked her to fill them out. In about twenty minutes a nurse called her name and asked her to follow to the examining room. "Please remove your clothes, Mrs. North and put on this gown," she said pleasantly. "The doctors will be in soon to examine you."

"Doctors?" she questioned silently. "Guess they work as a team."

The door opened and two men in white lab coats entered. The elder man, supposedly Dr. Tolbert, spoke first. "Good afternoon, Mrs. North. I am Dr. Tolbert and this is my partner, Dr. Burton. We'll both be seeing you, Dr. Burton is taking over my practice."

'How do you do," she said as they came to the side of the examining bed and helped her lie down.

Before they started the poking and prodding that she knew would come, they asked her lots of questions about her past medical history and the present situation. Then the examining started, and though the nurse was in the room, she was most uncomfortable having two men inspecting, what seemed to her, like every pore. They were very gentle and tried not to embarrass her, but she still shivered from within.

"Mrs. North, please get dressed and then come up to our offices on the next floor. The nurse will show you where it is," said Dr. Burton. He looked to be about forty, with prematurely graying hair and clear, blue eyes. He was not terribly handsome, but his gentle manner gave Patti a feeling of confidence.

The nurse went with her up the stairs to the next floor and showed her into a paneled office with pictures of birds lining all the walls. She recognized several of the artists and mentally complimented Dr. Tolbert on his taste in art.

"Mrs. North, you are probably aware that you are pregnant, is that not true?"

She took a deep breath. "Dr. Tolbert, I guess I knew there could be a chance, but I really didn't think that's why I have felt so strange the past few weeks."

"Well, congratulations, my dear. It looks like you are about four months into your pregnancy. As it sometimes happens, you still had periods in the beginning. This is not to be a concern, but with the pain and spotting you have been experiencing, Dr. Burton and I feel you should take it extremely easy for the next few weeks to prevent a miscarriage. Now we know you are new here and want to know if you intend to continue with us for care."

Patti was trying to take in all he was saying, but she still had this feeling of disbelief. "I was planning to stay in Kersey, at least for six months, but now I don't know what I should do. Also, I just accepted a job teaching art at St. Mary's School two days a week. Will it be alright to do that, doctor?"

"As for the teaching, if you feel alright and if the bleeding stops, by all means, take the job. It will be good for you. But as for staying in Kersey, only you can make that decision."

Dr. Burton wrote out a list of vitamins she should take and gave her a brochure on *Pre-natal Care for the First Time Mother*. He told her to make another appointment for early next month. She paid the receptionist, in cash, and feeling like she was in a fog, found the door. The nurse called out to her and catching up, handed her the packages from the department store. In her surprise and confusion, she had left them under the examining table.

She thought she should go back by the Abbotts, but didn't want to talk to them about this yet. "I can call Priscilla from the pub when I get back to Kersey." She needed some time to sort this out and then she would call.

Patti went back to the tearoom, drank an entire pot of tea and sat staring out the lace-curtained window. "Oh dear, now this is really getting complicated. A baby." She smiled as she thought of all the months she had hoped for a day like today, and now that it was here she didn't know whether to shout for joy or cry in despair. The taxi rank was just outside the tearoom door and the driver... same one she had this morning... was sitting behind the wheel, reading *The Times.* She got in and put her packages on the floor.

"Well, looks like Mrs. Thatcher is sendin' out more signals of tax increases from Downing Street," he said as he folded the paper and started the engine. "Back to Kersey, 'ya be goin, miss?"

"Yes, thank you," she said as she laid her head back on the leather seat and closed her eyes. "A baby... my own baby..." she thought as she tried to fathom the news of the last hour. Then it struck her... *William.*

CHAPTER EIGHTEEN

THE RINGING TELEPHONE… caught William's attention as he opened the door to his plushly carpeted office. Catching it on the fourth ring, he said, "William North," and sat down firmly in his large, navy blue leather chair.

"Will, this is Joel. Think I've got a good lead on where Patti may be."

"Great. What'd you find?"

"Now, we're not sure, but from checking some information we got at the airline and then back to a small travel agency downtown, we think she went to East Anglia, Suffolk region, to a town called Sudbury," Joel said as he flipped through the North file.

"Where the hell is that?" William snapped.

"It's about an hour and a half by train from London. We traced her to a little hotel in South Kensington and the manager told us he thought she was going to Sudbury."

"Do you have anyone over there who can go get her?"

Joel, a bit surprised that William wasn't out the door himself, said, "Not at the moment, but we can hire someone if you wish. Just remember, the manager only said he *thought* that's where she was going. He was a bit guarded when my associate was questioning him… like he knew more but didn't want to get involved."

"Hell, did you offer him any money? That always works."

"Will, old boy, we don't have to operate that way. We can probably get all we need without that," Joel said as he laughed. "I'd suggest our next move should be to send someone to this town of Sudbury and see if any of the people there might have seen her. Don't think it's very big, shouldn't be too hard to do. By the way, you didn't get me a good picture of her yet. Think you can send one over today or tomorrow. And Will, this is going to cost quite a tidy sum. We'll need some travel advance for our representative."

"Yea, I'll get a picture from Mother and have it couriered over to you tomorrow morning. How much money you need for this rep?"

"About ten grand ought to do it," Joel said as he waited for the reaction.

"Ten grand… my word, Joel, where's he going to stay, *The Dorchester?*"

"Will, airfare, meals, taxis… all this adds up and you know how expensive it is in England. And, we don't know how long this will take. It could be two or three weeks."

"Okay, I'll send the check over with the picture. Let me know as soon as you have something really good and I'll be on the next plane myself. I want a piece of this action."

Now he was beginning to sound like the old William that Joel remembered from college days… tough, aggressive, ready for a fight.

The offices of Richman, Richman and Seigel were humming with usual legal activity that afternoon as Joel came out of his office and asked the dark haired girl to get Cliff Hackett on the telephone.

"I have Mr. Hackett on the line, Mr. Richman," she squeaked.

"Wish she'd take some voice lessons," he thought as he picked up the telephone. "Cliff, how've you been?"

"Fine, Mr. Richman. Got some work for me today?"

"You bet, Cliff. This could be a very interesting and lucrative assignment for you. Have your suitcase packed and your passport handy?"

"You bet. Where'm I going this time?"

"How does England sound?" he asked, knowing that Cliff would go just about anywhere for excitement… and money.

"Sounds good to me. When do I leave?"

"Cliff, come on in to the office tomorrow morning, make it ten, and let's go over all the details. This is a domestic project… guy's wife has left the country and he wants her back. I think you'll find it pretty challenging."

"Okay, Mr. Richman. I'll be in tomorrow at ten. Thanks a lot."

****

"William, please stop picking at your food like a little boy," Marian said, taking delight in her opportunity to do some *smothering.* "The cook took special time to make your favorite roast beef tonight and the least you can do is try it."

"Come on, Mother. I'm just not hungry. This whole mess with Patti leaving has me madder than hell and I'm just waiting for the day when I can confront her with what she's done to the family name."

William North, Jr., sitting at the head of the table, didn't utter a word, but silently ate his meal and watched the sparring between mother and son. Totally out of character for the normally passive man, he stood up and pounding his fist on the table, said, "William, you wouldn't be in *this whole mess* if you had paid more attention to that dear girl than to your friends. I could see her retreating more every day into a world beyond here."

"William," Marian shouted... she called them both by their first names. "What do you mean?"

"Just what I said," he answered, the veins on his neck bulging from rage. "She's done no harm to the family name. If anyone has blemished it, it's you, William, with all your shenanigans with those so-called friends of yours. All they ever want is the North money… in business and pleasure and you've seen to it that they've gotten a big share of it. I don't blame her for trying to find a better life. Sure, you gave her money, a big house, jewelry, the North name, but you forgot to give her what she really wanted in this marriage… your time and attention."

Mother and son, stunned by this sudden outburst from a man they had always known as calm, cool and always together, sat looking in amazement at his tirade.

"And further," he added, "if you ever do find her, and I hope you don't, I hope to God she never comes back here to this sham of a life. Why I have stayed in it so long, I don't know. I'm too old now to start over, but to Patti I raise my glass and say, BRAVO!" Satisfied with his announcement of displeasure, he fell firmly back down on his chair.

By now Marian was sobbing uncontrollably, and William, unable to believe what he was seeing and hearing, just sat there staring.

William North, Jr., the heir of the North fortune, and the one North who did not have the courage to change, accepted his station in life and did what was expected of him. All his life he wished he could do what he had expected of himself. Standing up again, he moved his chair away from the large mahogany banquet table and turned to go into the library for his evening sherry. Grabbing his chest, he gave a low moan, and fell to the floor.

****

St. Luke's was filled to capacity with mourners from all over the world... those who genuinely cared for the gentle William Lloyd North, Jr. and those who knew it would be good business to be there. Father Charles Downing Satterfield offered his best homily to give the deceased a respectful sendoff. Flowers banked every vacant space around the altar and the blanket of flowers on the casket covered the top completely. William held his mother's hand as she cried softly throughout the entire service and showed visible signs of grief himself. William, Jr.'s body was interred in the North family plot at Lakeside Cemetery. He'd probably have preferred cremation with his ashes strewn in some exotic place, one of the places he never got to visit but in his dreams. But the North's didn't do it that way.

A huge reception, second only in size to Patti and William's wedding, was held at Vandermere and attended by almost everyone who was at the funeral service. When William was asked by his friends about Patti, his pat answer was, "She's on a holiday in Europe and was in one of those out of the way places. We couldn't get in touch with her in time for her to get back for the service." The resentment he felt at her absence added to his growing anger and to make matters worse, he had not heard from Joel for almost two weeks. Seeing him at the funeral made William impatient to discuss the case. Midway through the reception he excused himself from his mother's side and went into the bar to find Joel… figuring he'd be in there trying to solicit business.

Just as he suspected, Joel was strong-arming one of North company's biggest clients and it was well known that this man used the services of the legal profession frequently to his advantage. "Joel, excuse me, but could you come into the library for a few minutes. I need to talk to you."

Joel slapped the other man on the shoulder. "See you later, Sam. Enjoyed hearing your story. Let me know if I can help you with that," he said as they left the room.

"Never stop *lawyering* do you, Joel?" William sarcastically said. "Let's go in here." They went into the darkened library and William turned on a light next to one of the leather sofas.

"Listen, it's been two weeks and I haven't heard one word from you. What is the deal?"

"Will, take it easy. I met with our rep and he left for England last weekend. Then your dad died and I didn't want to bother you. Just don't worry. We're working on it."

"Hell, I can't even tell her my dad is dead." He turned his head, not wanting Joel to see that he was near tears. "Now we'll have the will to probate and she should be here for that. I know the old man liked her a lot and probably made some special provisions for her. Not that she deserves a damned thing. This is the most frustrating thing I've ever been through. I'm a married man without a wife." With that he stormed out of the library and back into the bar. "Give me a double scotch," he told the bartender. He took the drink and went back into the ballroom to stand beside his mother, who by now was seated in a gold and pink brocade chair, surrounded by well wishers of varying degrees of familiarity. Most of the people there had spoken to her and she was glad to finally sit down. Some distant relatives, no doubt hoping for some inheritance, had driven up from Kentucky and were being most patronizing of her. Seeing William approaching, she was hoping for some respite from this seedy looking group.

"William dear, these are your cousins from Sardis, Kentucky. I don't think you've ever met them. Sally Mae and Rudy North, this is my son, William. Oh yes, this is their daughter, Delilah."

"Delilah?" he laughed silently. But, he definitely noticed how attractive she was... long, auburn hair, green eyes and a figure that bespoke of her sensuality. She filled out her knit dress to perfection and despite the heavy makeup, was a real beauty. "Nice to meet all of you," he said, looking only at the younger cousin. "Uh, can I get you a drink?" he asked, eyes still only on her.

"Dropping her head in a coquettish tilt," she blinked the green eyes and said,"Ah'd just love a glass of that there champagne."

"Oooo," he cringed, and thought, "she murders the King's English."

"Sure thing. Mother, would you or Sally Mae or Rudy like something?"

"Thank you dear, I'll just have a glass of cream sherry, please."

The other cousins said they'd follow him and choose something when they got there. He guessed they'd probably be looking for a beer or *bourbon and branch.*

They stood talking for a few minutes, William trying to think of conversation they would enjoy... or understand. Delilah turned to William and said, "How come a handsome dude like you don't have a wife?"

He laughed. "I do. But she's out of the country and we couldn't reach her in time for the funeral." How he was getting tired of telling this story.

"Well, if ya'll get lonesome up here, ya'll have to just come on down to Kentuck...we'll teach 'ya to square dance," she offered. Just what he wanted to do. At that moment he saw one of his college friends come in the door, one who had missed the service. Glad to have a reason to leave this *charming* group, he took his leave and went over to greet his friend.

****

Cliff Hackett asked the flight attendant for another bourbon and water, tuned his headset to the movie channel, and sat back in his First Class seat to enjoy the early part of his flight. Thinking to himself, "So I don't have a normal home life, but boy, is this ever livin'." He had long ago divorced, his wife not adapting to an absentee husband, and devoted himself to the life of a private investigator for high-priced law firms like Richman, Richman & Seigel. His assignments usually kept him in the States, but occasionally he was called for a foreign case and took good advantage of the perks that went with this type travel. Along the way, when it suited him, he found female companionship. Tonight he had his eye on a cute redheaded flight attendant. He liked watching her reach up into the overhead compartments for pillows… a lot of her leg showed. "Wonder if she has a London layover."

The plane made a rather bumpy landing and his briefcase slid out from under the seat in front of him. Picking it up and unlocking the latches, he took out the picture of Patti and studied it. Her blond hair, blue eyes, and nice smile showed the face of a supposedly happy person. William said the picture was taken on their honeymoon. "Most people look happy on their honeymoon," he thought, questioning again why anyone would want to run away from such an envied lifestyle. "Guess she must have had some good reason, now I gotta find her and find out why."

The cute redhead let him know she had a steady boyfriend and was not interested in *seeing London* with him. He deplaned, walked up the jetway and started through the long immigration and customs process.

CHAPTER NINETEEN

ROSES WERE BLOOMING... in every English garden this time of year... and were especially pretty in East Anglia. Sudbury's gardens in the houses in town were smaller, but each yard, no matter the size, had an assortment of rose bushes. Floribundas and tea roses, pinks and yellows, they all were peaking and Patti thoroughly enjoyed walking down the streets and lanes to view their beauty and drink in their fragrance. Kersey's larger yards made for less formal gardens, more casual in the arrangement of plantings.

"It's not the right time to plant roses now, but I will in the fall, and if I'm not here to enjoy them next summer, perhaps someone who appreciates roses will care for them," she planned. At least I'll have the fun of digging in the dirt and watching them get a start." Even though a large rose garden would have to wait, Patti bought some wildflower seeds and four small rose bushes at the market and made a garden beside the cottage. Someone had put up a wire fence on the property line many years ago and she hoped the sweet peas would find that a good place to grow and climb. Having visions of chicken soup with fresh herbs, she found a rocky area in the sun and put in an herb garden.

214

The smell of basil and rosemary lingered on her hands as she finished her digging for the day. "Guess I'll soak these weary bones in a nice bubble bath and make an omelet for my dinner," she thought as she stored her garden tools in back of the cottage. John had cleared an area and made a small lean-to so she could keep these kind of things out of the house. Television in this part of England, or in all of England for that matter, did not have much selection, and she had a difficult time understanding the English humor, so most nights she listened to music on the radio and read books. She finished her dinner… or as they say in England, her tea… and started filling the bath tub. Patti had felt unusually good the past few days and hoped the problems of last week were behind her.

The teaching job was going well and Tom was most considerate in keeping out of her way at times that could be awkward. She liked having mornings to herself and looked forward to the afternoons with the children. The regular teacher had planned to start a series on American artists, which was most convenient, so Patti had no problem following her teaching schedule. The children loved her and seemed totally mesmerized when she talked about the Wyeth family, Thomas Sully, Grandma Moses and others from the States. "I'm going to find some good books on American artists and leave them here for the children. Maybe I can get them in London," she thought as she reviewed her plans for the next day. The selection of resources in Sudbury was limited and she had not yet ventured beyond there.

Thinking it would be a good experience for the children to compare the works of English and American artists of the same era, she asked the school director if they could plan a field trip to some area where Constable had painted. He was born about ten miles southeast of Kersey in 1776, when America was fighting the British. "This should make for an interesting contrast in art," she laughed. "John Blake White would have been painting about that same time, and he did a lot of work based on famous battles. I can tell them about him. Oh, and John Trumbull was another of that time. How sad though to compare the tranquil scenes of Constable's English countryside with American artist's scenes of battles and generals surrendering... like General Burgoyne at Saratoga." The more she thought about the field trip, and it had been approved, the more excited she became.

With sixty children to supervise on a field trip she knew she would need some other adults to help. The director gave her a list of parents who frequently offered to accompany on field trips and she called until she had ten parents to drive and assist.

Much to her surprise Tom came by her class one day and said, "If you would not find it too presumptuous of me, I'd certainly like to go with you on the field trip. You just might need another pair of hands with all those children."

"That would be lovely, Tom. We're going to have the children bring a picnic sack and their tablets for sketching," she said. "I'll pack extra and you can share my blanket. Oh, Tom, do you know where the best place would be… that is, where we can sketch scenes similar to what we think Constable would have done, and then spread our blankets for lunch… maybe near a stream… trees… are you getting the picture? No pun intended," she laughed.

"I think the perfect spot might be a little south of Sudbury, near the River Stour. If you'd like, we could take a drive over there tomorrow morning before you teach and check it out. It's only about thirty minutes from here.

"Tom, that would be a big help. I never realized how inconvenient it is not having a car. Thanks so much. What time will you be by?"

"Pick you up at ten and we can pop in somewhere for a spot of lunch before I bring you back here to the church."

Humming to himself as he left the classroom, Tom went back to his offices for afternoon counseling appointments set up by the secretary. Patti finished with the third and last class, gathered up her papers and walked back to the cottage. She had warm feelings of anticipation as she thought about the venture tomorrow and wondered if the time might present itself for her to share with Tom her good news.

The little black car came down the drive promptly at ten and Patti was waiting on the steps. Tom got out and came over to open the door for her. "Looks like you've been making a garden."

"Yes, I planted some wildflower seeds, some herbs and four little rose bushes. Do hope they'll grow."

They took a back road, unpaved and dusty, to the B1508 south of Sudbury and drove in and out of some rather isolated lanes until he pulled far back into a field and stopped the car. "There's your perfect setting, Mrs. North," he said firmly as he helped her out of the car.

"You're absolutely right, Tom," she replied, looking at the field of wildflowers, a few, huge, old trees and a tired, vacant sheepherders shack. The sound of the river, running over rocks, could be heard and birds were sending their songs into the wind.

"The children will have so many scenes to choose from and we can put our blankets under those trees," she said, pointing to a cluster of knarled oaks. The sweep of grasses, tall as most of the children, would make fun places to hide if they wanted to play. "Thank you for finding this place. Have you been here before?"

Taking her hand and leading her toward the river, he said, "Yes, let me show you where I have spent many an hour in prayer and meditation."

They walked down a narrow path, the high grasses on either side, and came to a clearing at the water's edge. Several large rocks were in a formation reminiscent of a *Stonehenge* scene. He sat down on one of the smooth rocks and motioned for her to sit on another beside him. "Isn't this the most peaceful place you've ever seen?' he asked as he stared at the river.

"Oh, Tom, I can see why you like it here. The only sound is nature and it makes me feel like I'm a million miles from any other humans... except you, of course," she said with a laugh and a touch of sadness in her heart. "How can I tell him my news, when I sense his emotion at this minute," she thought. "Well, nothing ventured, nothing gained, and he is a friend."

"Tom... uh, I want to share something with you," she haltingly said as he threw some pebbles into the water.

"Is this that confession you wanted to make when we first met?" he said with a laugh.

"It might be interpreted that way," she answered as she contemplated how she was going to tell him without breaching their friendship. Taking a deep breath, she told him about her childhood, her parent's death, and her marriage to William. She described to him how overwhelmed she felt most of the time and how lonesome she was even with so many people always in their presence. And, she told him she got to the breaking point where she had to forsake the *Cinderella* life for something more simple. She told him that her friend's description of Kersey stuck in her mind and she finally made the decision to leave. She told him she had no idea what she was looking for and how long she intended to stay… even though her lease was for six months… and she told him she was happier now than she had been since she was a child. Then she told him she was pregnant.

Tom stood up, walked over to *her* rock, and knelt down in front of her. He took her hands in his and brought them to his lips. Caressing them gently, he smiled and said simply, "Patti." The adoration in his eyes was undeniable and he was unable to speak further.

Patti did not know how to respond. She felt so terribly confused and needed his friendship, especially now. But she could not deny also that she was very attracted to him.

"Tom, please help me. I cannot, and do not want to continue to live the life I had, but now I have an obligation. I had no idea I was pregnant when I left. Symptoms didn't occur until a couple of weeks ago. Now I find out I'm four months along." She kept trying to talk and make him understand that she had wanted a baby, but not under these circumstances. Tom just sat very still beside her, staring at the river.

Finally, after several minutes, he spoke. "Patti, life is never predictable, no matter what anyone says. Sometimes we reach for the stars, only to have storm clouds get in the way. Right now you're in the clouds. I apologize again for letting my emotions show through, but do know that I truly care for you and sympathize with your situation. I will stand by you as your friend and will not make you uncomfortable, I promise." His attitude suddenly became more as a counselor, or of the priest that he was. Pushing some of the graying hair off of his forehead, he sniffed and added, "You haven't asked my help, but as your friend, I think it wise that you make contact with someone in your family in Cleveland. For your child's sake, this is not the time for you to be alone." With even more tone of a priest, he firmly suggested,

"And, it might be a good idea for you to consider your husband."

She could see the hurt in his eyes, yet she had not given him encouragement and felt no guilt, even if she was attracted. Their conversation on the drive back to Sudbury was strained and mostly of a bland and cursory content. Tom stopped in front of a small tearoom near the train station, where the hourly train from Marks Tey had just arrived. Ordering soup and salad, Patti sat quietly counting the seams in the lace curtains. Tom re-read the menu four times and settled on a ham sandwich and a cup of tea. The tension between them was as tight as two spiders on the wrong web. Someone had to fall off. It was Tom who broke the spell.

"Patti, look, I can't just pop into your life and expect you to be there for me. You're right, I knew nothing about you, only that, I, uh… never mind. Anyway, as it seems I'm one of the few friends you have here, and I intend to help you in any way I can. If that means getting you back to the States, or helping you stay here. Whatever… I won't interfere, just tell me how I can help."

"Thank you, Tom," she said, feeling a great release of tension and grateful for his reassuring smile. "I just found out about this a few days ago and haven't decided what to do. I love it here and have found a peace that is unexplainable… you'd only understand if you had lived my life the past three years. Suffice it to say, there is joy in my soul for the first time in a long time. And thank you, Tom, for being my friend."

Their lunch arrived and as they were enjoying the more pleasant air of the day, Patti said, "Tom, have you ever met Charles Abbott, the Estate Agent for the Olmsteds?"

"No, but he might have attended services."

"He and his wife, Priscilla, live here in Sudbury and were so nice to me before I moved into the cottage. I'd love for you to meet them. Do you think we have time?"

"If we hurry. You have to be back at school in an hour."

"Oh, good. Their house is just three blocks from here."

Tom paid the bill and they got back into the little black car.

****

Cliff Hackett picked up his canvas bag and walked over to the tourist kiosk across from the train station. "You have any maps of this area?" he asked the elderly man sitting behind the counter.

"Yup, help yourself."

He put the maps in his bag and looked down the street toward the center of town. "Any place nearby to get some lunch?"

The man pointed toward the west and said, "Yup, two pubs next block, tea room across the street, hotel in town."

"He's sure a bundle of information," thought Cliff as he crossed over the street to see what the tea room had, though he would have preferred a pub and a beer. Forgetting to look to his right, not his left, when crossing the streets, he was almost knocked down by a little black car driven by a priest and presumably his wife. "Boy, I gotta remember to look the other way over here. Gonna get myself killed."

CHAPTER TWENTY

SHARING FRIENDS… was always something Patti liked to do, especially when they were as nice as Priscilla and Charles Abbott. Tom recalled that he had met them at one of the services several months ago, and lest he think they were backsliders, Charles immediately told him, "We go 'round to Holy Trinity in Long Melford, and me missus is head of the ladies league." Much larger than St. Mary's, Tom had attended meetings there many times. Its congregation was very wealthy, going back to the inheritances from prosperous wool and cloth merchants of the fifteenth century.

"Mrs. North," Tom said somewhat formally, "We best be gettin' you back to the school or they'll send the hounds lookin' for 'ya."

"Oh yes," she said, looking at her watch. She hugged Priscilla and Charles and followed Tom out to the car.

"Thanks for taking time to stop at the Abbotts. They have been so nice and I really like them. If I do have to go back," she said sadly, "I'll miss them… and you," Tom gave her a broad smile. "You'll make all the right decisions, I'm sure, Patti." They got back to the church just as the bell was ringing for the one o'clock class. She could hardly wait to tell the children about the wonderful place where they would be going on the field trip.

That evening Patti sat down at the desk beside the fireplace and tried to compose a letter to William. The words would not come. "Oh well, I'll try again tomorrow morning." Figuring a good night's rest would help, she put the paper back in the desk drawer and went into the bedroom.

Cliff Hackett checked into the Orwell Inn, named for a nearby valley. Located three blocks from the center of town, he knew it would be a good place to work from... "That is, if she's in this area." He had fish and chips in the pub next door and put down several pints of the local brew. He tried to find a television show to watch and settled on a rugby game. "Gotta get my game plan together for tomorrow," he thought, as he drifted off to sleep.

After a breakfast of porridge and toast, Cliff went into reception and asked the clerk if he recognized the girl in the picture... the one William had given to Joel Richman. He told the man she was new in town and might be leasing a house, or flat, or something.

"Right. You might want to check with an Estate Agent. They do the leasing 'round here. There's a couple of 'em on the next street."

"Thanks, buddy. I'll do that," he said as he went out to the sidewalk. It was starting to rain and he didn't have a raincoat or an umbrella, so he pulled up his jacket collar and started down the street.

"Guess I'll have to buy a darned raincoat. They say it rains here almost everyday."

"You seen this girl around here, by any chance?" he asked Charles Abbott as he walked into the office.

Charles, being the ever-calm man, slowly looked at the picture and said, "Why would you be wantin' to know?"

"I'm workin' for her husband in the States. Seems she's run away from home and he simply wants her back... nothin' real excitin'. You seen her?"

"Might have... 'n might not have. Can't be sure."

"Well, I'm stayin' down the street at the Orwell. If you remember anything, give me a call. Okay, buddy?" Cliff made some notes in a little book and started down the street to the next Estate Agent.

Soon as he felt sure the man was out of sight, Charles locked the office and made his way home. "Priscilla," he called out as he entered the cheerful house, "Quick, we have to go 'round to Kersey and find Patti."

"Charles Abbott, what you be so upset about?"

He told her about Cliff's visit and the picture. "I'm sure it was our Patti. We got to be helpin' her, no matter what that man says. Did she talk much to you regardin' her family or her husband?"

Tying the scarf around her head and running in the rain to the car, she tried to think on the conversations she had had with Patti. "Mostly we just talked a lot about lady things... her decoratin' the cottage and all that. A couple of weeks ago when she came by she was lookin' for a doctor. Seems she'd had some monthly problems and needed a checkup... or so she be tellin me," Priscilla said, holding tight to the door handle. Charles was driving much faster than usual "Do we have to be goin' so fast, Charles Abbott? Surely you'll be gettin' us killed 'fore we even get to Patti's."

As they turned into the driveway, they had to pull around to the side of a Range Rover parked next to the big house. "The Olmsteds must have come up for a few days," he said, continuing on to the cottage. Priscilla followed Charles to the door and they waited for an answer to their knock. A big smile on her face, Patti said, "How nice to see you two days in a row. What brings you to Kersey?"

Charles told Patti about Cliff Hackett's visit to the office. "Now Patti dear, we don't be meanin' to pry, but if you be in some kind of trouble, we'd like to be helpin' 'ya," Charles said, noting the fear growing in her eyes.

"Oh, Priscilla and Charles, I am so sorry. I haven't been entirely truthful with you, but I haven't committed any crime." She then told them the entire story, just as she had related it to Tom. When she was

227

finished, they both came over to the sofa and hugged her. Priscilla reached into the apron she had forgotten to take off before they left Sudbury and found a handkerchief. Wiping her eyes, she said, "Patti, you don't need to be a worryin'. We will be helpin' 'ya, just like 'ya was our own child."

Charles, trying to find the right words, said, "Right. Now first things first. Do 'ya want me to find that bloke and come here with him so 'ya can get this worked out? Said he was stayin 'round at the Orwell Inn."

"No, not yet. I suppose it's time I made a call to William. Tried to write a letter last night, but didn't know how to tell him the truth… that I really am happy and want to stay here. Oh yes, about staying here… I see the Olmsteds are in the big house. Thought I'd walk over and introduce myself. Actually, I was getting ready to do that when you came."

"Don't be worryin' about them," Charles said, "They don't need to be knowin' anything 'bout this right now. I'd suggest you just pay a friendly call and don't engage in talkin' 'bout the present situation."

"Oh, sweetheart," Priscilla cried, as she again wiped her eyes and blew her nose with a loud swishing sound. Her empathy touched Patti and she fleetingly thought of Mom Mead. "Guess I will have to call them, too," she thought.

"I don't understand the law in the States," said Charles, "But if 'ya think 'ya might be needin' the services of a good solicitor here, we can give 'ya ours' name. Don't see how anyone can make you come home, if you don't be wantin' to. But why would your husband hire a private investigator to find 'ya?"

"You just don't know William. He's used to power and always having his way. Oh, he can be quite charming... I was charmed... but underneath the handsome facade lies a devious man. I may be the first person to ever challenge him. His father, a nice enough man, but no backbone... inherited the business from his father and it was just expected that he run it. I always felt he probably would have been happier as a truck farmer or an accountant. When William finished college, his father literally turned over the day-to-day operations to him and then went into a mental and physical decline. He rarely spoke up to voice an opinion, but when the two of us were alone he was so nice to me. We had very interesting conversations and he told me how he would have liked to travel to the Orient... with a backpack. So out of character for this quiet man." Patti continued, feeling somehow compelled to share more with the Abbotts. "William's mother, Marian, was, as we say in the States, *a real piece of work.* She ruled the house and their social life strictly from her point of view and her desires. Our wedding was actually her wedding. I had very little say, but to please William, I went along with his mother's wishes. All I wanted was William. Little did I know that she would never share him with a wife. And he apparently loved the attention he got from both of us... and all of his friends. Finally, the *Cinderella Syndrome* caught up with me and I became very unhappy... and here I am."

Patti said she would call William as soon as they left... "Guess I'll have to use the telephone at the pub."

"No," said Charles, "You be comin' back with us, use our phone and let's confront that investigator bloke and get it over with, so you be havin' some peace."

This almost demanding order from Charles surprised Patti, but she was so glad to have someone telling her what to do. She never failed to respond to a fatherly figure, attributing that to the early loss of her own father. She got her bag and raincoat and started to get in the Abbotts car, when Charles suggested, "Why don't we be a stoppin' in to say hello to the Olmsteds. I need to talk with them for a bit about the lease."

"Okay," answered Patti, thinking another few minutes was not going to make much difference in today's situation.

****

"Harriett and Richard, this is your tenant, Patti North," Charles said, as they were invited into the well-appointed parlor.

"How do you do," Patti said, taking a seat in a brocade covered chair.

"Oh, my dear," said Harriett with a definite London accent, "We are so pleased with what you have done in the yard around the cottage. And the cottage looks wonderful. You have certainly improved that sad little house."

"Thank you," Patti said, feeling a sense of appreciation, "I'm on my way into Sudbury with Priscilla and Charles right now, but when I get back, won't you please come for tea and let me show you the inside. I love your little cottage and am so glad Charles was your Estate Agent. He and Priscilla have been more help than you can imagine," she said, giving them a rather cryptic, but meaningful smile.

Charles told Patti he was going to find Cliff Hackett and bring him back to the house. She agreed that would be fine and would wait until she spoke to him before placing the call to William. Fortunately for Charles, Cliff was in his room watching another rugby game and finishing up a pint of brew from the inn's dining room. He followed Charles as they walked the three blocks to the Abbott house, not saying much along the way. As they reached the front door, he asked Charles, "Is this lady afraid of me?"

"Why would 'ya be askin' that?" said Charles, "Did she do somethin' wrong?"

"No, just curious. This is just a domestic case and nobody in this town has heard anything about her... good or bad."

Cliff held out his hand to Patti and she did not respond, instead asked him to have a seat in the parlor. Charles and Priscilla stayed in the kitchen, but had a good line of sight to the parlor should she need them.

"Mrs. North, I represent your husband's lawyer. He's not happy about you leavin' and wants to know where you are. Now that I've found you, gotta let them know."

"Mr. Hackett, I will call William myself. I am over twenty-one and can travel if I please. Why on earth he is chasing me is beyond my comprehension. Now that you have found me, do me the courtesy of leaving here and do not try to contact me or these friends again."

Cliff walked alone to the door, tipped his head to Patti who was standing in the hallway, and called out good-bye to the Abbotts. She could only hope he would think she was living here and not try to follow her to Kersey. "That's MY place," she thought. "But I really don't want to put Priscilla and Charles in jeopardy." Discussing this later with them, they assured her it was not a problem and said they would never reveal where she really lived. People like *the ladies* were another story. She hoped this man would be satisfied that he found her and would get on the next plane to the States.

Priscilla pulled up a deep-seated chair to the telephone table, gave her a note pad and pencil, a kiss on the cheek, and left the room. Patti took a deep breath, and with great hesitation, dialed the operator. "I want to call collect to Cleveland, Ohio, in the States, please."

"May I have the number you wish to call and your name, please," said the operator. Patti waited for what seemed an eternity, and then there was an answer at the other end of the line. It was four in the afternoon in Cleveland and she hoped William had not left for a golf game.

"Good afternoon. William North's office," said the voice, one which Patti did not recognize. "This is Monica, how may I help you?"

"May I please speak to Mr. North?"

"Who may I say is calling?"

"This is Mrs. North."

"Mrs. North, Jr.?"

"No, Mrs. North the third," Patti answered, emphasizing the third.

Denoting a gasp and, "Oh, please hold the line, I'll get him right away," Monica put her on hold.

"Patti, you there Patti?" he said, a rapid coarseness in his voice. "Where are you? Patti, can you hear me?"

She was close to hanging up the telephone. "I can't," she thought, "now it will all be ruined. My little cottage, the garden, the Abbotts…Tom" He said her name again and she answered. "Yes, William, I'm here."

"Well, where the hell is *here*." he shouted into the telephone.

"Surely by now your "investigator" has called you and told you I'm in Sudbury, England."

She could feel the anger in his voice and began trembling.

Again he shouted, "I'm coming over on the next plane and you're coming back with me. Do you understand?" The non-compassionate North was stretching his wings… and his voice. "You are a North and you cannot abandon us like this. Patti, Patti, are you there?"

"Yes, William, I'm here. But please don't come here. I'm fine and need to have time to think."

"Think. What the hell about? Do you know what this escapade of yours has cost me in time and money? Not to mention the embarrassment when people inquire about you. What do you need to think about anyway? You have everything anyone could want…right here in Cleveland, and you leave it for some stinkin' little village across the ocean. And what are you doing for money? Your bank account hasn't been touched since you left."

She sighed and with much pain tried to tell him that she was teaching art on a temporary basis. He kept ranting and barely heard what she said... except the word "temporary".

"You bet it's temporary, babe. Get your stuff together, because you and I are going to have some things to talk about on the way back."

"William, I'm begging you, please leave me alone for a while," she pleaded, by now crying as well.

"Patti, I'm telling you one more time. You WILL come back with me." He hung up and threw his green marble, desk pen set across the room. "Monica, get my travel agent on the phone."

CHAPTER TWENTY-ONE

THE FLIGHT OVER... would turn out to be longer than he had expected, but probably that was due to his anxiety of finding and confronting Patti. Service in First Class was provided by four flight attendants who hovered over each customer to a point of becoming intrusive. After dinner he wanted to sip a brandy, study some information on Sudbury, and go to sleep. He had packed several client folders in his brief case and intended to make good use in Sudbury of any spare time he had while finding Patti. Thinking the Gainsborough Museum might give him leads on available art, he intended to work as well as pursue this latest cause. Though he knew Patti was in Sudbury, Cliff said he felt that was a front and she was living elsewhere. William was disgusted with Cliff's casual manner of learning her exact whereabouts and he did not like the recent additional expenses... "This guy must be taking a vacation on me."

Earlier in the week he had called Richman, Richman and Seigel. "Joel, this is William North. I want you to fire that Hackett guy and send him home. He's been over there two weeks, finds her in Sudbury, but doesn't know exactly where she's living. Can't this joker ask questions and find her?"

"Will, take it easy. These investigations take time. If you alarm the wrong people you don't get the information you want. He did find her, didn't he? Talked to her, too. And she called you from there didn't she?" asked Joel, sensing William's doubts.

"Yeah, she called me and begged me not to come over, but you know I said I want to be there to confront her, so I'm going. Anyway, I'm not funding anymore of this guy's vacation."

His deep sleep was abruptly interrupted as the flight attendant tapped him on the shoulder, handed him a hot towel and told him they would be serving breakfast in a few minutes. He looked at his watch and realized he hadn't changed it to London time, so pulling out the stem on the gold Rolex, he turned the hands to seven. "Oh, wow, it's only two a.m. at home, no wonder I'm still tired."

"Your breakfast, Mr. North," said the blond girl as she put the tray in front of him. Looking at food so early in the morning was not his usual start for the day. William's breakfast was normally a cup of coffee and a bagel or muffin. "'Spose I could get you to take this back and just bring me a muffin or something?" he asked as she passed by on her way back to the galley.

"Yes sir, Mr. North."

A quick trip to the bathroom and some cold water on his face made him feel a little better. Looking in the mirror he noticed that the strands of grey were increasing in his dark hair. "Guess I've earned those, considering all the details after Dad's death and now this fiasco with Patti." The anger rose in him again and he had a scowl on his face as he closed the door behind him.

"Good Morning, Mr. North. What's so unpleasant?" asked the blond flight attendant as he passed the galley.

"Oh nothing, I was just thinking about the hassle of going through customs and immigration. Shame somebody hasn't invented a way to speed up the process."

William took his seat and in a few minutes they were hitting the runway at Gatwick Airport. He went through the slow process at customs and immigration, wishing he were on the course at Vandermere, and went outside to find a taxi.

"How do I get to a little town north of here called Sudbury?" he asked the driver of the sleek black taxi.

"Don't believe I rightly know, sir, but you best go to Victoria Station and they can advise you. Want me to take you there?"

"Yeah, that'll be fine."

William leaned his head back on the leather seat and remembered the last time he was here. It was on their honeymoon and he made a good deal with several galleries in the city. Those paintings sold well back in Cleveland. He also remembered their first night in New York as husband and wife... and how he tripped over her slip... and how angry he got with her...but how sensuously and lustfully she became when they made love. "Perhaps I haven't been the husband she wanted," he pondered, going over the past three years piece-by-piece, day-by-day. Then he recalled the past few weeks being badgered by his friends as to her whereabouts. That humiliation attacked his manhood and he felt anger ooze back into his mind. "Oh, when I find her she is going to be so sorry."

The travel agent wasn't much help with directions to Sudbury, couldn't even find it on her map, so he was grateful for the taxi driver's suggestion of going to Victoria Station. The information desk clerk explained the departure times, track and offered to escort him to the ticket window. He thanked the lady, found his way to the window and went searching for a place to get a cup of coffee, since he had an hour to wait for the train to Marks Tey. The coffee was good and hot and helped him revive. He bought a *Herald Tribune* and turned to the financial pages. Several of the investments his father had made were floundering and it now rested on William's shoulders to make some changes. Marian refused to get involved in this part of their life, but she continued to lead the social circle for Cleveland, spending the money these investments made. "Ha," he thought sarcastically, "Patti doesn't even know Dad is dead."

As the train made it's way north, William watched with interest at the scenes, reminiscent of so many paintings they had sold through the gallery. Recalling that he was approaching Constable country, he thought, "Maybe I can find an agent here to help me get some good quality Constable prints. Those would sell well, I'll bet." He gave credit to Patti for arousing his interest in the Victorian artists... this was one of her favorite periods of art. "She's probably in a dream world here," he laughed.

The train pulled into Marks Tey and the two-car train was waiting for them to board. "Good thing it's warm today," he thought, as he looked at the open windows. Scanning his tour book, which he found in the book department at Higbee's, he read that the trip from Marks Tey to Sudbury was 11 3/4 miles "through landscape straight out of Constable's paintings." Trying to make the best of this frustrating situation, he sat back on the hard, cracked, leather seat and watched the farmlands, fields and valleys roll by. Half-way there they passed a clearing beside the River Stour. He saw a large group of children and adults who appeared to be having a picnic. Some of the children were running among the tall grasses and others were walking on the rocks in the shallow part of the river. "That looks like fun," he tought, with some longing to return to childish ways.

William slung his Hartmann bag over his shoulder and walked across from the Sudbury train station to an information kiosk. The elderly man behind the counter slid his glasses down on his nose and said, "Be needin some help?"

"Yes, can you tell me where I might find a nice hotel for a few nights?"

"Yup, the Orwell Inn is four blocks that way," he said, as he pointed to the west. "Better take that taxi over there," again pointing with his crippled hand, "Your bag looks a mite heavy."

"Thanks." He put two dollars on the counter and hoped the man had an exchange close by. "Oh yes, have any maps of this area?"

"Yup," he answered as he handed two to William. "And thanks."

Waking the driver from his morning nap, William threw his bag on to the back seat and got in the little blue car with the magnetic taxi sign on the side. "Take me to the Orwell Inn."

"Right. Been there before?" asked the sleepy man.

"No, just arrived, first time here. Say, would you possibly remember driving for this lady?" and he showed the driver the picture of Patti taken on their honeymoon.

"Yup, that'd be Mrs. North. She uses our taxis a mite more than most. Don't believe she has a car, she don't."

"Pay dirt," thought William excitedly, "Where do you usually take her?"

"Oh, I don't know that I should be givin' information on me customers to a stranger. Why you be wantin' to know about Mrs. North?"

"Listen, I'll pay you well for any thing you can tell me. I'm her husband."

"Right. But I could lose me license... and me car... if I do that without me supervisor sayin' it's okay. Have to check with him, I will," he said, hesitating.

"Okay, okay," William said, agitated that the driver wouldn't cooperate. "Can you find him now and ask him?"

"Oh no, he's out of the district for today. Buyin' a new taxi for us, he is. I can talk with 'im tomorrow, maybe."

"Well, would anyone else here in town know anything about where she might be?"

"Matey, I can't rightly tell 'ya. Don't know where she goes when she's here."

Burning with rage and frustration, he got out in front of the Orwell Inn and asked the driver to come back for him tomorrow morning at nine. "And have his permission," he demanded. "I'll pay."

It was close to noon and William was beginning to feel the lack of sleep invading his body. He checked into the Orwell, "No I never seen that lady," said the desk clerk when the picture came out of his passport case, and he took the lift to his room on the third floor. The Orwell was as near a luxury hotel as he would have expected in this town and he realized why Hackett's expenses were so high. "Why do I feel like that jerk took me?"

He hung up his clothes, brushed his teeth, which by now felt like they had feathers growing on them, and fell into the bed. William slept for ten hours. Getting up and noticing that it was dark outside, he felt hungry and wondered where he could get a meal at this hour of the night in this small town. The desk clerk said the dining room had closed at nine, but the chef was still there working on tomorrow's specials. William went into the paneled room which was dark except for some low lights over the bar. "Hello there," he called out as the chef looked up. "'Spose I could get a bite of late dinner. Got in at noon and slept longer than I'd planned." In a few minutes the chef brought him a bowl of barley soup and some hard rolls. With a pint of the local beer, this satisfied William, and he vowed to have a good breakfast in the morning.

He went back to his room, there was not any sign of nightlife here, and watched a rugby game and an English comedy. "That's funny?"

he thought. Hoping that a hot bath would help him relax and get back to sleep, he ran a tub of water. "Patti probably loves this," he thought, remembering her fondness for bubble baths in deep tubs.

The taxi was waiting in front of the inn and William jumped in with anticipation of some good news. "Well, did he say okay?"

"Nope, he said it would be somethin' like a breach of confidentiali... something, I don't be rememberin'. Where you want to go?"

"Nowhere now," William angrily replied as he got out and slammed the taxi door. "I'll just walk around and talk to people I think she might have met... do my own research." The driver waved and drove down to the taxi rank in front of the department store.

He stopped in several shops, showing Patti's picture to the clerks and owners, none had seen her, or were not sure. Some he felt were being very cautious, maybe thinking she was in trouble. Turning in to the department store he saw two ladies giggling as they looked at a magazine. Seeing him, they put it under the counter and smiled, as he got closer. "Morning, ladies. I was wondering if you have seen this lady?"

"Oh my. that's Mrs. North," squealed Cynthia as she passed the photo to Margaret. "Isn't she the prettiest thing?"

"You know her?"

"Why yes, she's a good customer of ours. We've probably sold her everything she bought for her little house, we did," said Margaret proudly.

"Her little house?" he asked.

"Right. She be leasin' a little cottage in Kersey, down the hill from the pottery it is," offered Cynthia.

Trying to contain his delight in hearing this, he asked, "Could you possibly give me her address, I really need to contact her."

"Oh, we couldn't be a doin' that you see. It would be interferin' in our customer's privacy," said Margaret as she sensed something strange about this conversation. "Cynthia, I think we best be gettin' back to unpackin' that order in the storage room. Come along."

Feeling that he had made some good progress, "How big can this Kersey be?" he went out to find the taxi driver.

****

Seeing dust rising from the drive, Patti looked up and saw Tom's car. She ran out the door and waved as he pulled in next to the cottage. "Oh Tom, thank you so much for yesterday. I think the children... and their parents... had a wonderful time. Some of the sketches they brought back are marvelous and you really need to nurture those students. Sorry about the runny egg salad, I should have

245

had Rosie make the lunch. Oh, I'm just talking like a magpie, but I has such a good time. Please, come have a cup of tea."

They sat at the little gate-leg table and discussed the events of yesterday over and over. She glowed as she described some of the children's reactions. "They all seemed to appreciate the day so. Don't they get to take field trips very often, Tom?"

"Patti, it was you. Your enthusiasm made this a very enlightening experience for them... one they will remember for a long time. Someday they will realize how you opened their eyes and minds to seeing art in an entirely different light. Do you know how special that is? By the way, the sandwiches were a bit loose, but they were good. Rosie's aren't, I've tried them. Her tuna salad is much better."

Patti was enjoying sharing with Tom the memories of the picnic and was aware of his attempt at being friendly, but reserved. She liked his warm manner and his appreciation for nature, children and friendship. He lived his profession, maintained his humanness, yet she wondered why he had never married.

"Patti, have you made any decisions yet?"

"We really didn't have a chance to be alone yesterday, Tom, or I would have brought you up to date on my dilemma. The Abbotts were here the other day. Seems a man had come around asking about me and showed Charles my picture. They took me to their house and the man, a private investigator, said William was looking for me and wants me to come home. I knew I had been found," she continued, "so I called William and tried to tell him to leave me alone. He got very angry and belligerent and said he was coming to get me on the next plane." She started to cry. Tom reached over and put his hand on her shoulder.

"Patti, do you want to go with him?"

"NO," she said loudly. "I want to stay here. At least for a while longer. Oh Tom, what shall I do?"

"I told you it has to be your decision. And, I've been praying for your courage in making that decision."

Wiping her eyes on her napkin, she looked longingly at him. "Tom, I do want my baby, but I am so unhappy back there. Why is life so complicated?"

They both turned as they heard a car come up the driveway. A blue taxi that Patti recognized from Sudbury stopped in front of the cottage.

Patti grabbed Tom's sleeve and gave a low moan as she sunk to the floor.

"Come in," Tom called, as he picked Patti up in his arms and carried her to the bedroom.

247

"Well, isn't this a cozy little scene," said the tall, well-groomed man who had come through the door. "And a priest yet."

CHAPTER TWENTY-TWO

RAGE AND ANGER... filled William's dark eyes as he saw Tom leaning over the bed where Patti was lying totally still. He pushed Tom aside as he stood looking at his wife.

"I'm Father Beacham," said Tom, reaching his hand to William, "and I do believe you must be William North... the third," he said with a slight tone of sarcasm.

"Yeah, I'm William. What's wrong with Patti... and what the hell are you doing here?"

"We were discussing the children's field trip of yesterday... she teaches art to our students... and when she saw you get out of the taxi she moaned and passed out," he responded, while wondering how to avoid a confrontation with this obviously very angry man.

"Did she tell you I was looking for her?" William said as he looked around the room, noticing her taste in decorating... the taste she never had a chance to exercise in Cleveland.

Tom went to the end of the bed and stood looking at Patti. "Here, let's cover her and I'll go to my office and call the doctor." He unfolded a blanket that was on top of the armoire and carefully spread it over her. Patti made no movements and this frightened him. He started out the door. "We'll probably have to take her round to his office in Sudbury. I have a car if you will allow me to help."

"Oh, uh, yeah," William said as he stared at Patti. "Has she been sick?"

"I think you best be discussing her health with her and the doctor. I'll be right back, my office is just up the hill." He closed the door quietly and got into his little black car.

Patti stirred and opened her eyes. "William," she gasped, "what are you doing here?"

"I told you I was coming to bring you back home. Didn't expect to find you sick. What's wrong anyway? Can I get you something… uh, water?"

"No, thank you. Where is Tom? I remember having tea with him before I passed out," she softly asked.

"He went to call the doctor and said we'd probably have to take you in to Sudbury. Patti, what's going on? Is this why you ran away? Are you sick?"

She did not want to tell him the truth just yet. "No, I'm not ill." Maybe it's something I ate at the field trip picnic yesterday," she said, trying to delay the issue. "I'll be okay, but guess it's a good idea to let the doctor look at me."

She sat up and pulled a pillow behind her back. William was walking around the cottage looking at the home she had made. He was impressed with how comfortable and unpretentious it was, yet revealing the brightness and airiness of each room. "See why you like it here. This is a quaint village and this cottage is cozy… almost cozy enough for two," he said as he watched for her reaction. "And so close to the church."

"William, I know what you must be thinking and you can stop right now. Tom is just a good friend and the rector of the church I attend… nothing more. He has helped me with several things, mainly gave me the job at the school."

"Seeing the look in his eyes when he looked at you sure seemed more than just friendship."

"Shame on you. He's a minister and he was here on behalf of the school. We were talking about the field trip. Don't you discuss customers with your secretary?" she said as she started to get out of the bed. Suddenly she felt a warm trickle of blood on her leg and holding on to the bedpost, she made her way to the bathroom. William had gone into the kitchen and did not see what was happening.

"Oh no," she thought, "Am I miscarrying?" She took care of the situation and came in and sat on the sofa. "William, I think I'd like a cup of tea. Could you put the kettle on, please."

"Gotten to be a real Brit, haven't you... with your *cuppa*," he said with a bit of mockery in his voice.

"You know I've always liked tea, William. And can't you be pleasant?"

"Pleasant!" he shouted. "Do you know how much in time and money this escapade of yours has cost me? Not to say anything of the embarrassment for the family. Mother gets ill every time someone asks where you are, especially when Dad died."

"Your father died? When? Why didn't you tell me?"

"Tell you? How could we, when we didn't know where you were. You are so stupid," he answered. "It was the night I found your letter. He went into a tirade... but you'll be happy to know it was in your defense," he said with sarcasm. "As he left the dining table and headed for the library he had a massive coronary attack and died. That old man really liked you, Patti. He said some very wise and astute things about you and me... some things I've been thinking about... like us trying to spend more time alone." His strange change in attitude was totally out of character and made Patti question his motives and sincerity. The teakettle was whistling. William opened some cabinets hunting for the tea bags.

"They're in the top right cabinet," she said, watching him clumsily trying to make a simple cup of tea.

She had finished half the cup when Tom's car came down the driveway. "William, here's Tom. Now please be civil... he is just a good friend and a very fine man. Could you get my raincoat out of the armoire, please," she asked as she gingerly stood up from the sofa.

Tom knocked on the door and cautiously pushed it open. "You must feel better. Good. I called the doctor and they can see you as soon as we can get there, if you're ready to go now."

"Yes, Tom, and thank you." She put on the raincoat, with some help from William, and they got into the little black car.

Dr. Tolbert had taken the afternoon off to attend a medical society luncheon and bridge tournament. Dr. Burton was taking all calls and the waiting room was full. *"See you as soon as you get there,"* she laughed to herself. Tom and William did not have much to say on the drive to Sudbury, save for William asking him about the history of Kersey. In the waiting room they spoke not at all, reading the out-of-date magazines. Patti put her head back against the wall and tried to think happy thoughts.

"Mrs. North, the doctor will see you now. Follow me, please."

"Good afternoon, Mrs. North. I understand you fainted today and passed some blood," he said as he motioned for her to sit up on the examining table. "Let me ask you a few questions and then we'll have a look and see how that baby is doing."

Lying on the table, Patti appreciated his gentleness and ability to make her feel comfortable. The examination was quick and he asked her to come to his office after she dressed.

"Mrs. North. I don't see any cause for concern, however, I must caution you to still take it easy. Stay in bed as much as you can for the next two weeks and then come back in and let's do another examination. You need to rest… not just your body, but your mind. From what you just told me, this has been a traumatic day. Do you want me to talk to your husband now?"

Thinking that might be easier than telling him herself, she said, "Yes, that would be good. I haven't told him I'm pregnant and maybe hearing it from you first might ease the situation. He's very angry right now."

The nurse called William's name and took him to Dr. Burton's third floor office.

"How do you do, Mr. North? I'm Dr. Burton."

"Hello, doctor," William said, thinking, "are all the men here handsome. First her rector, now the doctor." He'd never felt jealous before. This new reaction puzzled him.

"Mr. North, you realize, of course, the confidentiality between a doctor and the patient. Mrs. North has told me of the present strain in your marriage and has asked me to share with you information on her condition. She's going to have a baby."

"You're kidding," William bellowed. "When? When did she find out? Is this why she passed out today?"

"Just a minute, I'll answer all your questions. First, let me say that your wife is in good health, but needs bed rest for a few weeks and then she must continue to take it easy for the next five months. You should be having a son or daughter in late November. I would suggest she not do any heavy housework or take any extended journeys until the birth."

"Oh, that's impossible, doctor. You see, I'm taking her back to Cleveland as soon as she can get packed. She left and I want her back home," he defiantly said.

"You don't understand, Mr. North. Your baby's life is dependent on your wife maintaining a quiet lifestyle until the birth and that would exclude long trips... especially an eight-hour flight to the States. It's out of the question, I'm afraid. Also, any emotional strain can be harmful to her pregnancy. A mother-to-be needs care and love, free from worry, to carry and deliver a healthy child."

William protested. "I'm sure you're right, doc, but I'll get her home and then she can have the best care money will buy. Cleveland almost has more doctors than you have pubs," he laughed.

William stood up, reached out to shake Andrew Burton's hand and left for reception where Patti and Tom were waiting. As he opened the door and saw Patti's questioning face, he said, "Well, it seems we have another North to add to the family tree." He put his arm around Patti's shoulder, giving her a gentle squeeze, and led her to the outer door.

"Congratulations, William," said Tom as he opened their doors.

"Yeah, thanks," William snarled as he got in. "Guess this is when a guy is supposed to be happy. That of course would be if his wife wanted to live with him."

Patti was crying softly and dreaded being alone… *dreaded being alone with him…* when they got back to the cottage. Tom said good-bye and, "I'll pop 'round tomorrow morning to see if you need anything, or need a ride back to Sudbury or perhaps Chelsworth. You might enjoy seeing the thatched cottages and gardens in Chelsworth. William, one of your countrymen wrote a nice book about Chelsworth, *Suffolk Summer*. His name was John Appleby, an

American soldier stationed in Suffolk during World War II. Spent his entire free time here bicyclng 'round the area. He said it was the prettiest village in England, but we like to think the prettiest is Kersey."

"Thank you, Tom," Patti said as she patted him on the arm. She would have, under other circumstances, hugged him in appreciation.

William just made a gesture of a wave and grunted something under his breath.

Tom had barely left the driveway when William started into a shouting tirade berating Patti for her relationship with him. "I don't care what that country doctor said, you're going to pack up and we're heading back to Cleveland tomorrow. You start packing, I'll walk over to that pub and get us some dinner. Or do you want to eat there?"

Crying again, she sobbed, "I don't want any dinner. I just want my baby and I won't be forced into going back until the doctor says there's no danger." The hurt she was feeling brought back memories of the emotion she felt when her parents died. "William, why don't you just be honest and admit that it's not me you want, but another William Lloyd North."

"Wait a minute, Fair Lady. I didn't even know about this baby thing until today. I came to get you… like it or not." He slammed the door as he left and kicked stones in the driveway as he walked to the pub.

Paddy Houlehan was wiping the bar when William came through the door. "Hullo there. What can we be 'gettin 'ya to quench tha thirst?" he said as he put a beer glass on the counter.

"Oh, a glass of your draft ale will be fine," William answered as he surveyed the old pub.

"Aye, a pint of me best ale fer 'ya," he said as he drew the golden brew. "Don' think I been seein' 'ya round here. 'Ya visitin?"

"Sort of. I'm William North and I've come to take my wife home."

"Oh, you must be Patti's husband. Nice lady, she is. Almost nice as me Rosie. Why 'ya be takin' her home? She's takin' a big likin' to us here and that children love her most, they do."

"Well, I've always believed a wife's place is beside her husband, not halfway around the world," he said with a sound of power and authority.

"Aye, 'ya be right 'bout that, but sometimes it be best to take some time away. Good for the soul it 'tis," retorted Paddy. They got into some discussions on Kersey, art, and the state of politics in the United Kingdom. William was beginning to get hungry.

"Can you pack up two orders of fish and chips to go?"

"Sure and I can, Mr. North. Now you be tellin' Patti we send our best. She been so busy with tha children that she hasn't come round the pub lately."

When William left the cottage Patti threw herself on the bed and sobbed in anguish. "I will not go back now. He can't make me leave. What am I going to do?" She fell into a deep sleep and did not hear the door open when he came back with two sacks of fish and chips for their dinner. Not realizing she had slept for two hours, she was also not aware that he had downed several pints of Paddy's best ale while bending his ear. Only his slight stagger gave her the hint that this was not a good time to confront him with her decision to stay.

She kept the dinner conversation light, telling him about her pleasure in fixing up the cottage, John Dunthornes' help, and *the ladies* who knew everything she needed. "Oh, I met them. They sure are funny little women... like two old twins," he said.

Now she knew... "He found out where I was from Cynthia and Margaret," she thought. "Oh well, he'd have found me somehow anyway."

Patti cleaned up the compact kitchen and went in to start the water in her tub. As she started to take off her slacks and sweater, William came into the bathroom. He took her in his arms and kissed her arduously, though the smell of all the ale he had drunk made her nauseous. She responded to his warmth and truly wanted his love. But the hurt he had inflicted on her today was beyond denial. He led her to the bed, she protested that she had to turn off the water, and they slowly sank into the feather-topped mattress. Somehow he was different in his approach to meeting her needs… "was he being so gentle because of the baby," she wondered, "or is this some devious way to make me want to go back." Later his snoring kept her awake and she watched the moon chase clouds in the summer night sky. "If only he could always be so gentle. If only we could be HERE together, and not in Cleveland. I must keep my wits about me and not let this one lovely night sway my thinking."

She woke to the smell of coffee, "How did he know where it was?" and getting up, put on her silk robe.

"Well, good morning, Fair Lady. Thought you might sleep all day and we need to get a move on. Ready for some coffee?"

The hot coffee hit bottom, as she knew she could not avoid telling him that she was not going. A strong wave of nausea hit her and she ran for the bathroom. William followed her, held a cold cloth to her forehead and helped her back into the bed when the sickness passed. "Gosh, I'm sorry you feel so rotten. Do you think you can eat some breakfast?"

"William, sit here," she gestured toward the side of the bed. "I have to tell you something, and please hear me out." Patti took a deep breath and asked God to give her the right words. "I am not going back with you now. Give me time to think this over and to feel better. I will come back. This is your child, too, and I cannot deny you this experience, but you must give me the understanding that I need right now. Will you?"

She could see the veins on his neck quivering and she knew he was growing impatient. "Patti, only because you are so sick right now will I even think about this. I'll give you a month and I'll be checking with that doctor. Also going to talk to Mom's doctor and get his opinion. You WILL come home and the sooner the better."

Patti wanted to show him her appreciation, give him a hug, but she could not bring herself to touch him now. In her eyes he again became the dictatorial man that she left in Cleveland. She merely looked at him and said, "I guess that's fair, William. I'll try to make it as soon as I can so we can make arrangements for the baby's birth."

He walked down to the pub and hoped to get a call through to his travel agent... with a flight home tomorrow morning. What he would tell friends and family would come to him in time. For now he just wanted to get back to the States and his business. Since William North, Jr. died the gallery had endured falling sales. William attributed this to his involvement clearing up his father's affairs and trying to find Patti. As he crossed over the swail he remembered the Gainsborough home in Sudbury and thought about going there to see if he could make some purchases. Paddy started pouring him an ale as he entered the door. "Oh, no Paddy, I need to be seeing about some business today and if I get to drinking your great brew, I'll never get it all done."

"Oh Mr. North, you be takin' a bit 'o time now to enjoy the ale. That business will wait. Americans rush tha day too much... need to make time to sit with 'ya friends, 'ya do," Paddy said as he pushed the glass toward William who was now sitting at the bar.

In between two pints, William made the call and was confirmed on the noon flight out of Gatwick. Taking the early train from Sudbury to London would get him there in time. "I might even find time to take a quick taxi to Christie's in Kensington, if I'm lucky," he said, always thinking of the gallery and possible business.

Patti heard the purr of the little black car as Tom pulled into the driveway. She came out onto the stone steps and greeted him, a smile on her face. "You look mighty happy for a lady in a dilemma," he said, as he got close, wanting to put his arm around her shoulder. He hesitated and instead gave her a brotherly pat on the arm. "Must have some good news."

"Well, Tom, we've sort of reached a compromise. I told him emphatically that I would not leave now, but considering the baby, I will come home soon. He gave me a month. Now if I can just get stronger in that time. Dr. Burton doesn't want me to travel at all."

Tom had a sad look on his face, as if he had lost something very precious. Patti stared at him and taking a deep breath said, "Tom, we'll have a month together, that should make you smile."

What she said opened his heart for hope. It wasn't said like a friend who was leaving, it had undertones of a lover offering encouragement. He hoped it was the latter, but felt the guilt with that hope.

William made contact with an art agent at the Gainsborough museum and the man took his order for some of Gainsborough's prints... he didn't want any *Blue Boys*, but some of the less popular landscapes that the artist so loved to paint. He took the little blue taxi back to Kersey, stopping to *tip one more pint* with Paddy and then walked back to Brett Lane and the cottage. It was almost dark and he could see Patti in the kitchen.

"Aren't you supposed to be in bed resting," he asked as he came in the door.

"Oh, William. I was beginning to worry. Where have you been all day?"

"Been in Sudbury orderin' Gainsborough prints and had me a pint wit Paddy on me way home," he said in a mock English way.

She laughed and continued to stir the lamb stew on the stove. "I've made a lamb stew for dinner. Are you hungry?"

"Hungry for you," he said with anticipation in his voice as he came over and picked her up.

"William, the stew is ready. Put me down," she squealed as he dumped her on the bed and began to take off her robe. The other William was present and his rough attack caused her to pull back.

"Don't pull away from me, you little bitch. You're my wife and I want what's mine. Bet if I was the rector there you wouldn't be pulling away," he snarled as he tore off her gown.

"William, I've told you, Tom is just a friend, and my word, he's a priest. Please stop, you're hurting me."

The stew got cold on the stove and that night Patti again watched the moon chasing clouds. Her body hurt and she knew she was in trouble.

CHAPTER TWENTY-THREE

STRANGE DREAMS... were running through her head when she awoke to the sound of a car going down the driveway. Patti ran to the front door, just as the little blue taxi was turning on to Brett Lane. She went back into the bedroom and saw no evidence of William's belongings. "How nice. He brutally hurts me and then leaves without even saying good-bye."

Turning back toward the living room, Patti saw a note on the table. Her eyes searched as she hoped for kind words. Instead "the old William" prevailed and left his message to hurt.

> *Patti,*
>
> *Glad you're so happy here, but you have one month to finish your folly and get back to Cleveland.*
>
> *Thanks for your hospitality.*
>
> *W*

She put the note down on the table and slowly walked toward the bedroom. "How can he be so cold and mean...'thanks for the hospitality.' I sound like a Bed & Breakfast, instead of a wife."

Ache and nausea wracked her body as she recalled the incident of William subduing her last night. What she thought might be a change in his attitude and affections turned out to be a cruel and sadistic display of his need to be in power and control. "How could I have been so naive, he'll never change. But for my child's sake I must figure out some way to play the game… at least until the time is right to make some drastic changes."

Three years living as a North had taught her how they think and act and she knew they… not just William… would never let her take the child away. "Seems I remember Scarlett saying, *"I'll think about that tomorrow."* And that's what I'll do. Today I'm going to rest, drink tea and read a book." She was glad he was gone and really didn't care that he left without telling her.

Drawing a tub of warm water always made her feel good, and as the bubbles increased in size, she gazed on her reflection in the mirror. "Oh, my word. He bruised my face," she cried as she saw the blue marks on her cheeks and neck. "This was the man I loved… but the life I had so wanted came upon me with little warning or preparation. It was too perfect and too much. Now I suppose I must pay for my lack of exploration and experience." She stepped into the tub, hoping to soak away the bad feelings of last night, and let her thoughts drift to babies, a subject she had not given much thought to in her young life. The day passed pleasantly and at dusk she got out of the bed, by now strewn with magazines and books, and made a light supper of scrambled eggs and toast.

Mornings became afternoons and afternoons turned into long nights. Patti did not teach for two weeks and deliberately stayed away from the church… and Tom. With the exception of a few trips into Sudbury for groceries and reading material, she stayed near the cottage. Some mornings she trimmed the roses, remembering Dr. Burton's advice to be very careful lifting and pulling. Television did not offer much, but she looked forward to the daily news, finding it reporting rather than editorializing as in the States. On a very warm summer day at the end of July, Patti decided to walk to The Street and go into the pottery. "I think I'd like to get some cache pots for ivy. I could put them on the kitchen window sill." She followed the stone path and came to the showroom door. Choosing two pots with the familiar blue design, she looked around for someone to help her. "Hello, is anyone here?"

"Well, Mrs. North, how are you bein' today?" said Robert Barrows as he wiped his clay laden hands on his canvas apron.

"Fine, Mr. Barrows. Just want to pay you for these pots."

"Say, if you still be interested in workin' a bit I could use a body for a couple 'o days."

"Mmm, would I have to be standing all day?" she asked, thinking of Dr. Burton's warnings.

"Oh no, we been needin' a body to pack some boxes for shippin'. You'd be sittin' at a bench for 'bout four hours a day. Don' be payin' much, but you might find it interestin'."

She surmised that this might meet with the doctor's approval. "Okay, I'll take the job. When do you want me to start?"

"Well I know you teach in the afternoons at the church. Would 'ya be likin' to work Tuesday and Thursday mornins?"

"Great. I'll see you next Tuesday morning. Nine okay?"

"Right. Thanks, Mrs. North."

"Patti, please," she said as she stepped back on to the stone path.

Suddenly a panic that went all the way through to her stomach caught her and she thought, "Oh no. William said I had one month and then I had to come home. Well, I'll just ignore it for now and get on with it." She stopped at the swail and watched the ducks splashing water on the stonewalls, thinking how peaceful it was in Kersey and how very sad she was going to be when she left. Turning around, she decided to visit Rosie and Paddy in the pub. "Maybe they'll have some cold lemonade," she thought as she realized how thirsty she had become from the walk. The Houlehans were happy to see her and inquired about her health. "I'm feeling fine and last night my baby moved for the first time. That was a real thrill," she told them, wishing deep down she had felt differently about William... different enough to want to share that thrill with him.

"Oh, Swee'heart, that's wonderful," Rosie said as she came around from the bar to give Patti a hug. "You're gonna be a fine mother, you are, Patti." Glancing toward the door, she called out, "Good mornin' Father. Can we be gettin' you a lemonade, too?"

Tom, looking cool even on this warm day, his eyebrows shooting up when he saw Patti, said, "Well, hello dear friends. Yes, I'd be lovin' a glass o' your lemonade, Rosie. 'Tis a warm day out there and I been chasing six year olds on the soccer field. They love to make a tired fool of the old rector here," he laughed as he pulled out a chair next to Patti. "So good to see you, Patti. I apologize for not comin' round, but know you wanted to rest and would you believe I was elected to fill in your place. Can you be imaginin' me, the art dummy, tryin' to teach those children about the finer things in art. What a sight it must be."

They all joined his laughing, and with an effort, Patti broke her silence and said, "Tom, I've missed seeing you... and the children," she added. I'm doing much better now and can come back to the school next week, if you'll be having me."

"Yes, yes," he enthusiastically responded. "We sure do need you. Say, since it's so hot today, why don't you let me take you round to the cottage."

"That would be nice." Torn between desire and reality, she fought off the compulsion to add an invitation to tea, feeling unsure of her own self-control.

As they turned into the driveway, Patti relented and put her hand on Tom's arm. "Tom, would you like to come in for a cuppa? I'd like to talk to you about something."

Not wanting to create a situation they would both regret, he said, "Patti, do you really think that is wise? I remember how adamant and unyielding your husband was regarding your return to the States and I had a most definite feeling that he didn't like me spendin' time with you. I don't want to be makin' things difficult for you when you return to your family."

"Why can't we just be honest? She said, her voice in a high nervous pitch. "I've had to be the perfect society wife and I'm miserable. Do you think God wants me to be unhappy for the rest of my life? Sure the baby complicates things, but..." she hesitated, said a prayer for courage and forgiveness and said, "Tom, I think I'm in love with you and I know you have feelings for me. There, I've said it."

The tea in the cups had long since become cold. Tom and Patti sat on the sofa, his arm around her shoulders as he looked lovingly into her eyes. "Patti, dear. Now that we both have stated our sentiments, where do you suggest we go from here? You have to go back to Cleveland and have your baby. I have to stay here with my church. And under all of this, it is wrong for us to even speak of a future together. God forgive me, but I do care for you and I do want to have a life with you, but right now I cannot see through the haze."

"I've given this a lot of thought, Tom, and this is what I plan to do. Next week I'll go back to Cleveland. After the baby is born I'll give William full custody and then I'll come back here."

"Patti," he shouted, "You cannot possibly be thinkin' such a thing. That is your child you are carryin' and it needs a mother. I don't believe this is the Patti I love sayin' this, and I surely don't take it as flattery that you be choosin' me over your child. I'll not be a part of this." Standing up, he went to the door, looked back at her as he shook his head, and walked out to the little black car. She didn't see him again and didn't return to the school.

She spent most of the next week crying as she packed up her clothes. She sent a note to the Abbotts, told them she hoped they would come to see her in the States, and asked their understanding of her decision to leave. She told Charles that she wanted to leave the furnishings she had bought for the next tenant. "I hope they'll enjoy living here in this peace as much as I have." The roses were blooming prolifically and she picked a large bouquet to add fragrance to the cottage for her last few days. Purposely avoiding contact with people she had met in the village, and apologizing to Robert Barrows at the pottery, "I really need to go back to Cleveland and have my baby there,", she set about closing up the cottage. It hurt... to put away the tea kettle from which she had had many a cup of tea, to close the curtains and darken the rooms, to set the ivy pots outside, hoping for nature's watering, to store all the garden tools in the lean-to John had built, to take in the chairs where she had sat under the trees so many days, and to make that last call to the taxi company.

"Perhaps this hurt is my punishment for expressing my love to Tom. Now he, too, has guilt where it should be love. What a mess I've made." Patti wept as emotion flooded her soul.

The little blue taxi stopped in front of the Sudbury train station and she heard the two-car train coming down the track. She paid the driver and thanked him for all his past courtesies, then went into the small station office to purchase her ticket. The conductor announced boarding and she found a seat... the same one where she had sat that first trip when Tom was with her. The whistle blew and they started down the track. Patti stared out the window and looking out over the

272

parking lot, she saw the little black car. There was Tom, waving for as long as she could see him.

The rest of the trip was very tiring for Patti and she was sorry for not planning to stay a day or two at the Tramore in South Kensington before continuing to Cleveland. Indulging herself, "For the baby," she bought a ticket in First Class and enjoyed the pampering enroute. She called William's office and told the receptionist that she would be arriving at three that afternoon and hoped he could meet her. She did not want to talk to him on the telephone. The memory of his last night at the cottage was still quite vivid and she did not want to endure a trans-Atlantic confrontation.

Filing through customs and to the outer glass doors, Patti tried to find William, sure that he would be there. As she stopped and turned to look around, a uniformed chauffeur called her name and rushed up to take her carry-on bag. "Good afternoon, Mrs. North. I'm Peter. Mr. North asked me to meet you, sending word that he was in a most important meeting at the Vandermere. Said he would see you this evening for dinner."

"Vandermere, my eye," she thought. "That *important meeting* was probably chasing a little white ball over eighteen golf holes with three friends. Oh well, better get used to being alone in a crowd again."

Marian wasn't at home either. In fact, there was no one there except the cook and she was busy calling in an order to the butcher. Patti thanked Peter for taking her bags to the suite and offered him a tip, which he graciously refused. "No need, ma'am. The Norths take good care of me."

"I'll bet they do," she laughed to herself, as she went into the spacious bathroom to undress and think about a shower and a nap. Longing for one of her delicious bubble baths, she made do with the hot shower. There was a nice breeze coming in the bedroom window, the day being unseasonably cool for Cleveland in early August, and sleep came swiftly as she dreamed of the cottage and her peace.

"Well, well, Fair Lady has returned to her castle," William said sarcastically as he pulled the sheet from her sleeping form.

"Hello, William," she said slowly, as she yawned and sat up. "It was a very tiring trip and I needed a nap. What time is it here?"

Looking at his Rolex, he said crisply, "It's nine in the evening and dinner is being served downstairs. Are you going to grace us with your presence?"

"Oh, William, do you have to be so nasty?" she bravely asked, considering the fact that she could tell he had been drinking.

"I'll be anything I want to be and don't try to be the charming little wife we know you detest being… maybe being a rector's wife is more your style."

"That's not fair. I'm here, aren't I?"

"Yeah, but for how long? And don't get any ideas about leaving again. That baby is going to have a mother and father who live together… well, in the same house." As he started out the door, he turned and said, "Guess I should ask how you're feeling."

"Better, thank you, though the doctor was not very happy about me making the flight over." She marveled to herself that he even asked.

Dinner was strained. Marian was more formal than ever and showed no interest in England or the cottage. She only asked health questions and informed Patti that her doctor's appointment with the family obstetrician, Dr. Norman Weatherly, was made for tomorrow morning at ten. "And Patti, I have several maternity outfits waiting for your fittings at Christina's maternity boutique. The nursery is being painted in pale green and the furniture will be delivered next month. My decorator is making the curtains and I've ordered several layette items. The bridge club is having a shower for you and there are four others planned by some of our close friends," she droned on and on.

Remembering the words of a western song, *Back in the Saddle Again*, Patti just sighed and resigned herself to the past role she played. "At least I'll have the baby to concentrate on and Marian can't be there all the time," she thought, as she accepted the fact that her life would not be her own... not here.

"Patti, have you had any unusual pain or bleeding in the past?" asked the white haired Dr. Weatherly.

"Yes, I spotted several times and did have some pain. I also fainted a couple of times, but my doctor in Sudbury told me to rest a lot and I did. Is there some problem with the baby?"

"Well, I can't be sure, but the size concerns me. By now your baby should be quite a bit bigger. You did say you have felt movement, didn't you?"

"Yes, last month. But it hasn't moved a lot since then," she answered, feeling anxious and fearful.

"Now don't get worried. We'll run some tests, do an ultrasound and I'm sure everything will be fine. However, it's a good idea to continue to follow the rest suggestion. And Patti, don't have relations with your husband until we get the test results. I detect some fragility in your ability to carry this child and we want to make sure you go to full term."

As she got off the examination table, she thought of his last statement. "That's going to be interesting, considering William's idea of marriage."

That evening, when they had gone to the suite, she told William what Dr. Weatherly had said.

"You mean I can't have my wife until she has the baby?" he snapped, "Is that my passport to other avenues?" he said with a smirk on his face. "This might be an interesting pregnancy after all."

Glaring at him, despising his coarseness and lack of sensitivity, she said, "I know you're hurt... no, your ego's hurt... that I left you. But you have your ways to be happy and I wanted a chance to find mine. Why do you have to be so controlling?"

The veins on his neck were enlarging and twitching and she feared an all too familiar scene. "Don't tell me what I am. And what did you find, Fair Lady, but a man of the cloth to comfort you."

"Please, William. Let's not ever discuss Tom again. He was just a friend and my minister. I've told you that several times. What can I say to make you believe me?"

Kicking his shoes off as he went over to the bar, he poured a stiff drink and came over to sit beside her on the bed. "Here, have a sip, it'll do you good."

"No, it's not good to drink when you're pregnant."

"Oh come on," he said as he pushed the glass to her lips.

She pushed his hand away and started to go into the bathroom. He threw the glass across the room and shoved her to the bed, then started to rip her blue gown from her shoulders.

The eerie noise of the ambulance's sirens broke the silence of the night. Dr. Weatherly was waiting in the emergency room as the medical technicians gently wheeled in the gurney. Patti's grey face was looking up at him and she gave him a faint smile as she closed her eyes.

CHAPTER TWENTY-FOUR

STREAKS OF PALE LIGHT... were finding their way into the darkened room at St. Vincent's Hospital where Patti lay in a coma. Dr. Weatherly was on the staff here as well as at the private clinic in Shaker Heights, but felt the facilities here were more conducive to caring for Patti's condition. Marian was not pleased with the choice, but because of the circumstances, she backed away from any confrontation.

"Dr," the nurse spoke quietly, "Mrs. North's blood pressure is almost normal. Do you want to continue..." Before she could finish he interrupted.

"Miss Lanier, this patient is in extreme danger and I do not want you to leave her side unless you have a replacement. The blood pressure is not the main concern here. She is fighting losing her child as well as the emotional and physical injuries she has sustained from last night. Please let me know any change in her condition. I'll be in the doctor's lounge writing some notes."

Ellen Lanier returned to her chair near the bed and watched Patti's slow breathing. Her head had patches of bandages and her face was bloated and bruised. "How could a man do this to a woman... a woman pregnant with his child?" She took Patti's pulse and recorded it on the chart. Checking the fluid bag hanging on the side of the bed, she charted the large amount of blood. Just as she was about to adjust the oxygen flow, the door of the quiet room opened and a Cleveland police officer entered.

"Good morning. I'm Officer Donnelly and I've been sent to take some pictures of Mrs. North. Is that okay?"

"I'll have to check with Dr. Weatherly. One moment please." She went to the door and in a soft voice called to one of the nurses at the nurse's station next to Patti's room.

"Please page Dr. Weatherly and ask him to come here. Thanks."

The officer was trying his best not to make noise as he got his camera ready for the photographs.

Ellen, watching him curiously, said, "Guess you have a lot of gruesome pictures like this to take in your line of work."

"Well, it's not any worse than you having to take care of these poor people. Can't believe that guy could do this."

Dr. Weatherly greeted the officer. "I suppose it's necessary for your to do this, but we cannot let you touch or move her."

"Thanks, doctor. This isn't the favorite part of my job, but in cases like this we have to have proof of injury. What time last night did this happen?"

"We're not too sure, but think it was near midnight. Apparently he had been drinking and got quite violent... well, that's obvious, isn't it."

Officer Donnelly finished taking the pictures, packed up his camera and thanked them. "You'll probably be hearing from some detectives today, too."

"Yes, I suspected that. This is serious, and given the people involved, there will most likely be a lot of investigating on this one."

Two detectives arrived that afternoon and spent an hour asking Dr. Weatherly questions about Patti and other Norths he had treated. They told him that William was out of jail on bond, having been charged with assault and attempted murder.

"He's repeatedly denied that he intended to hurt her and that in her condition she lost her balance and fell against a marble table."

Dr. Weatherly, who had known the family since William was a child, remembered his temper tantrums in the dining room at Vandermere and later his encounters with the law when several times he'd wrecked his car while under the influence. He silently admitted that William was highly capable of last night's abuse.

"Thanks for your time, Dr. Weatherly. We'll be in touch with you in a few days." They left as quietly as they arrived.

281

Patti stirred and moaned deeply. Dr. Weatherly, who had not as yet left the room, leaned down close to her face. "Patti, can you hear me?"

"Mmmm," she smiled slightly and reached her hand up to his face. "I hurt." Each word given with effort, she continued. "Doctor... is my baby... alright?"

"Patti, right now your baby is trying to enter this world, but we're doing our best to let him stay where he is for a while longer. Would you like a sip of water?"

Again she smiled and gave him a look of sad, but deep gratitude. "Dr. Weatherly," she said in a muffled voice, "I don't want to see William... or ever go back to that house. Please don't let them make me go," she pleaded as tears ran down her bruised cheeks.

He took her hand. "Patti, you're safe here and we're going to take good care of you. Now you try to sleep, your baby needs that. Miss Lánier or I will be in the room with you." She closed her eyes, the sad smile still on her face.

The next few days Patti improved, but they would not let her use a mirror. The bruising on her face and neck had blackened and Dr. Weatherly felt the emotional strain of seeing herself in such a state would manifest in her physical status. The baby's birth was still in question. "We're trying some new drugs to restrain the delivery, hoping to delay this birth for another two months at least," he told the Meads, who had been outside her room from the first day of her confinement. Their first knowledge of the beating came from a radio report and they immediately went to the hospital. Helen told the doctor that they were all the family Patti had and gave him the entire story about her trip to England... and why she went.

Still not allowed to get out of the bed after two weeks in the hospital, Patti was getting impatient to go home. "But I want to go *home*," she said to Helen and John, "Not to the North's. I want to go to my home, with you."

"Honey," John said as he gave her a gentle hug, "Your room hasn't been touched since you left. We'll just move a crib in there and anything else you might need."

"Oh yes, it will be so nice to have you back, Patti," Helen said, avoiding reference to the baby as she was not yet certain of the prognosis.

Marian had been to see her once. She came two days after the incident, brought a huge bouquet of roses, and talked to Patti as if she had merely endured a tonsillectomy. Her nervousness was most evident to Patti as she chattered on about the bridge club and the latest dinner dance at Vandermere.

"You will have to get a pretty new outfit for the Memorial Day party, Patti. Christina's just got some exquisite summer maternity clothes. I'll have her send some over for you to look at. Oh, and the showers for you will still go on... I'll take pictures if you can't be there."

Patti put her head back on the pillow and looked up at the insulated ceiling tiles. "Doesn't this woman ever deal with reality? Some things never change," she thought as she watched Marian fidgeting in the cold steel hospital chair.

"Oh, I do wish they had sent you to the clinic. The rooms are so much brighter and the furniture is certainly more comfortable," she exclaimed as she stood to leave. "Now, Patti, if you need anything, just call. Peter can always drop things off for you. Oh, I must go. I have an appointment at the hairdressers in half an hour. Take care, dear." She patted Patti's hand as she brushed past the bed.

"Strange," Patti thought as she recalled Marian's visit. "She didn't mention William once and she usually can't have a conversation without bringing him into it at every other sentence. Interesting."

After two weeks in intensive care, and another two weeks on one of the medical floors, Dr. Weatherly told Patti he was releasing her to the Mead's care. "Abiding by your wishes, and from what I've learned of this whole situation, I think it wise that you go to the

Mead's. Now you must come back here twice a week for the next two months. We want you to deliver a healthy baby."

She was grateful for his understanding, and even though he was the North's physician, she felt confident that he was truly on her side. He had guided and counseled her regarding the trial which would be in another month, suggesting she make notes on the three years of the marriage. And, he offered to be with her at the trial.

John Mead had found a lawyer for Patti who was willing to go up against the North family. A graduate of Emory School of Law in Atlanta, Tyler Ford, was from an old southern family whose roots ran as deep in Georgia as the North's did in Ohio. He thrived on this type law and felt confident he could get a conviction. William, of course, had Joel Richman representing him. Joel was as cunning in the courtroom as William was in acquiring art. They both excelled. Now William needed Joel's unique ability of portraying him as one character, when he actually was another. Somehow he had to hide his dark side from the court. For the first time in his indulged life, William felt vulnerable and powerless. He knew he had beaten Patti, but he didn't actually remember that entire night. His biggest concern was getting a clean slate and getting the baby. He was determined to use every bit of influence and any amount of money to have his child. "She's not going to have my son... or daughter, Joel," he told his lawyer friend. "She provoked me to all this. Can't you build our case on that?"

"Will, old man. Her provoking still gave you no right to injure her… and possibly your child," responded Joel in a most matter of fact way. "What does the doctor say about the baby?"

"Aw, I don't know. He said there's some possibility of injury, but we won't know until it's born." This stark awareness of the seriousness of the situation caused him to sit bolt upright in the blue leather chair in Joel's office. "My word, if that baby is damaged she's really gonna pay."

"Wait a minute, Will. You're the one who did the damaging. Patti was the recipient of your anger. That's a hard, cruel fact and you'd better get used to hearing it 'cause her lawyer is going to pound away at it, I can assure you."

Day one of the trial William was noticeably uncomfortable and avoided looking at Patti or her lawyer except when Tyler Ford approached him and started the "pounding away". As the week dragged on each lawyer brought in character witnesses and each lawyer felt confident of winning. The jury returned a verdict of guilty for William, but recommended leniency due to his stress of Patti's departure and trip to England without informing him. He was not required to spend any time in jail, however the judge, an old friend of the North family, fined him and forbid him to have any contact with Patti. He said any custody issues would be solved in divorce court, since William was suing Patti for divorce and planned to ask for full custody of the child.

The strain of the trial took its toll on Patti and at the end of her eighth month of pregnancy she went into labor. She had been sitting at the kitchen table, helping Helen string beans for dinner when a tremendous spasm permeated her abdomen and she bent down to the floor, screaming in terrible pain. Helen called out to John, "Dad, get the car out of the garage and help me get Patti in, she's going to have this baby soon." Evidence of the birth process lay at Patti's feet and she tried reaching for a kitchen towel to wipe up the puddle. "Here now, child," said Helen, "You just get in that car and I'll get your bag. Glad you packed it last week. Wait, John," she screamed into the yard, "I've got to call Dr. Weatherly." John was helping Patti get her swollen body into the car, gently tucking a blanket around her, as the October chill had reached Cleveland. Helen ran out of the house and got into the back of the aging car. Patting Patti on the shoulder, she silently prayed that all would go well.

Dr. Weatherly met them at the same emergency room door where Patti had been wheeled in so terribly injured two months ago. "At least she's walking in this time," he thought to himself as he looked for an orderly and a wheelchair. With the help of his nurse assistant, they got Patti into the labor room and ready for what they hoped would be routine, despite the past circumstances and despite the lack of a full term pregnancy. Helen and John Mead waited in the room usually inhabited by nervous fathers. "Do you think we should call William?" Helen asked as she watched John add cream to his third cup of coffee. They had been waiting for six hours.

"Why in thunder would we want to call him after what he did to our Patti." John was not a forgiving man when it came to hurting those he loved. He loathed and detested William and all that he and the North's represented, but he never faulted Patti for her choice in marrying him. "That's hers to bear."

Dr. Weatherly came through the double glass doors, twiddling his glasses in his hand and seemingly in deep thought. He looked toward Helen and John and motioned for them to stay seated. "Mr. and Mrs. Mead. We have a bad situation here."

Oh, is Patti alright?" Helen cried, wiping her tired eyes.

"Patti will be fine, but the baby is very weak and we may lose her."

"A little girl," said Helen as she sobbed and turned to hold on to John.

John, his throat tightening up with fright, said, "What seems to be the problem with the baby?"

"We're not quite sure, but her breathing is poor and her blood isn't circulating properly." Then, with a great deal of hesitation, he added, "She also has some evidence of injury from the beating... some brain damage. We won't know for a few days how severe."

"May we see Patti," they both asked, almost in unison.

"Yes, but just for a few minutes. She's had a hard labor and we want her to be as still as possible for now. Also, we're not going to tell her the extent of the baby's problems for the time being." He led them to Patti's room at the end of the hall. As they entered, Dr. Weatherly called her name and she opened her eyes. "Patti, your folks are here to see you. I'll be back in a few minutes."

"Have you seen the baby?" she asked, her throat hurting from the methods of the past few hours' ordeal. "Is she pretty? They said they were doing some tests and I could see her later. Is she all right? Oh Mom, tell me, is there anything wrong?" She was crying and Helen reached for a tissue to wipe her eyes.

"Well, we don't know, Patti. Dr. Weatherly said he'd talk to us more later, but they want to check her out good 'cause of your trouble." Helen didn't lie too well and she hoped Patti would not see through her effort to conceal the truth. John calmly patted Patti's arm and gave her a kiss on the cheek. "You best rest there, little mom. We'll be outside if you need us," and he took Helen's arm and led her toward the door.

As they were about to close the door, Patti said, "I'm going to name her Rose... she'll be pretty like those in my Kersey garden."

The Meads went home late that night, still not knowing the condition of the baby... Rose.

CHAPTER TWENTY-FIVE

"ROSES ARE RED... violets are blue, my baby's here, now what will I do?" thought Patti, as she waited for the nurse to bring her breakfast. She had not yet seen Rose and was filled with anxiety. Dr. Weatherly was "on his way in," the nurse told her as she set the tray on her bedside table. The oatmeal and hot tea were unappealing and the thought of eating did nothing to calm Patti's nerves. "When am I going to be able to see my baby," she again asked the nurse.

"Mrs. North, I'm sure Dr. Weatherly will be speaking to you about the baby in a short time. Now you just have some breakfast to help get your strength back." She left the room and Patti glared at the tray of food.

She saw the bassinet first and then Dr. Weatherly who was pushing it into the room. "Oh, Rose," Patti said as she tried to get out of the bed.

"Wait a minute, young lady. You get right back in there. I'll bring this little girl to you."

Picking her up as if she were a satin pillow, he gently handed the pale, pink bundle to Patti. "Rose, this is your mother," he said as Patti reached out her arms for the baby.

She stared at the angelic sleeping form and brought her close to her own face. Rubbing her cheek against Rose's, she whispered, "Welcome, dear Rose. I'm your mommy and I love you so. We're going to have a wonderful life, you and me."

Norman Weatherly, usually a very calm and professional man, had tears in his eyes. "Patti, don't... don't get too attached. Your child has some serious problems and we're not going to be able to keep her with us."

"Oh, no. That can't be true. Look at how perfect she is... she can't be sick." Sobbing in anguish, Patti unfolded the blanket from around the sleeping child and studied her body, counting the fingers and toes, turning her over and stroking her soft skinned back.

"I'm afraid it's true. We've had some of the best specialists analyzing the situation. We don't know if this is a result of your unpleasant experience, or if it's entirely congenital. At any rate, she doesn't have the capacity to survive beyond a few days. I'm so sorry, Patti." He came over, sat on the side of the bed and put his arm around her shoulder. Kissing her on the forehead, he said, "I'll leave her here with you for a little while. She probably won't cry, but if you notice her breathing change, ring for the nurse right away."

As she watched Rose sleep, Patti prayed. "Dear God, for all the things I've done wrong, please forgive me, and let my baby live. She doesn't deserve this. Please God, please." Rose stirred and gave a very slight cry, so soft that Patti hardly heard her. She opened her eyes and gave a semblance of a smile. Her tiny head was covered in pale gold hair and her eyes were deep blue. Patti clutched her to her chest and cried, "God, you can't take my baby. Please don't take my baby."

By now Patti was crying uncontrollably and the nurse who was coming in to take Rose back to the nursery called out for help.

"Mrs. North, I've come to take Rose back to the nursery." She reached to get the child and Patti pulled away from her grasp. "Please let her stay with me."

"I have to take her back. Dr. Weatherly wants to perform some more tests. Please, Mrs. North, let me have the baby."

Patti handed her to the nurse and buried her head in her pillow.

Dreaming of being in the Kersey garden with Rose, Patti was awakened by a knock at the door. "Come in."

A police officer entered, followed by William. "Good afternoon, Mrs. North, I'm Officer Sherman. The judge has authorized that Mr. North can visit you and the baby. We hope you don't mind. Mr. North wants to see his daughter."

"I don't want him near my baby!" she screamed as a nurse came in.

"What's going on here, officer," the nurse asked as she came over to calm Patti.

"Ma'am, we have an order from the judge that Mr. North can see his daughter. He also okayed him speaking briefly with Mrs. North."

"Please step outside and I'll let you discuss this with her doctor." She motioned for them to follow her, stopping at the nurse's station to page Dr. Weatherly.

Norman Weatherly was torn between his remembrance of Patti the night of the beating and his present vision of a father wanting to see his firstborn. "Only because you have written permission for this visit will I allow it. Mrs. North has had enough trauma and emotion to last a lifetime. And I suppose you know the child is dying."

"Dying," gasped William, "What's wrong with her?"

"Surely you must have some idea why this child would not be right, given the past circumstances," Dr. Weatherly said with anger in his voice, yet not fully responding to the question.

"Oh, God, no." William buried his head in his hands and began crying.

"We don't have a final diagnosis, but the prognosis is simply that her body cannot sustain life. I'm sorry, Mr. North."

William stood looking through the nursery window, his body trembling. Facing the child, who looked perfectly normal, he bowed his head and again cried. "Guess I'd better say a few words to Patti."

"Hello, Patti." William walked halfway into the room.

"Hello, William," she said sternly. "Did you see our daughter?"

"Yeah, she's beautiful, just like you," he said remorsefully.

"I've named her Rose."

"That's pretty. I like that. You need anything, Patti?" His patronizing manner was not acceptable to Patti and she let him know.

"Don't try to be nice to me, William. I've endured all the North *pleasantries* that I care to. And you can tell Marian to stop sending me *things*. I don't now, or evermore need your help. You gave me enough." She turned her head to the window as he left the room, his head hung down and his shoulders bent… he looked to her like a very old man.

That afternoon at four o'clock Rose North drew her last tiny breath.

****

A cold, October drizzle came down on the grave site. Under the green canvas canopy Patti sat with the Meads and some of her college friends. The North family respectfully sat to the back and gave her no acknowledgment of loss… not that she felt they would. The minister finished his short homily, and before the small white casket was lowered into the wet earth, Patti placed on top a bouquet of pale pink roses. Baby Rose would rest next to Cassie and John. Helen and Glen Mead, on either side of Patti, helped her to the car and sat in silence as they drove back to the Mead house, each of them remembering the tiny babe who so briefly touched their lives.

****

"Mom, think I'll just rest here for a while," Patti said as she sat on the porch a few days after the funeral.

"Child, it's cold out here. Don't you want to come inside and Dad can build a fire?"

"No, I'll keep my coat on. I just want to sit here by myself." She pulled her coat tight around her still swollen stomach and sat on the old porch glider. Slowly moving back and forth, she started to sing some lullabies... ones she had learned in England, and hoped to sing to Rose. *Sleep on little baby, Mum's by your side. Sleep on little baby, don' be a startin' to cry...* Patti sang softly.

"Little Rose, you'll always be in my heart."

One morning, as Patti was helping Helen clean up the kitchen, they were talking about when she would start to look for a job. "I know I have to find something to do. After the divorce is final I'll get serious about it. I'm not asking William for a huge amount of alimony, though Tyler's friend said I can surely get it."

Tyler, who practiced criminal law, had introduced her to Edward Laing, a collegue who excelled in domestic law and was unafraid of taking on the powerful North family. Laing would be representing her in the divorce case. "I don't want to be obligated in any way to the Norths. I only want what is fair for the time we were married."

"Patti, you might want to reconsider, especially after what he did to you and..." Helen stopped mid-sentence, not wanting to say Rose's name. "Oh, I forgot to tell you. While you were in the hospital we had a very strange call. It was from some lady in England."

"England," she exclaimed.

"It was a very bad connection, but I think she said her name was Cynthia Files"

"Files? Oh, that was Cynthia Stiles, from the department store in Sudbury. Remember me telling you about those two cute, little ladies who helped me so much?"

"Maybe that's what she said. Yes, Stiles. Anyway, she asked for you and I really hesitated to tell her you were in the hospital, but she said she knew you came back to Cleveland and she wanted to tell you her friend, Margaret, was coming to Cleveland next month."

"Did she say where Margaret would be staying, or leave a telephone number?" Patti asked excitedly.

"No, as I said, I could hardly hear her. She did sound pleased to hear that you had had the baby. That was before Rose..." and she couldn't finish the sentence. "Said something about telling the good father... what did she mean by telling *the good father?*"

"She probably meant the rector at the church where I taught... Tom Beacham. Did she say anything about him?"

"No, just said she'd have Margaret call you when she got here."

Reflecting on the conversation, Patti thought, "Well, now Sudbury and probably Kersey will know I had the baby... but they won't know the rest." She thought about Rose and started crying.

A month later Glen called Patti to the telephone. "It's for you, Patti. Lady has an English accent... can't understand a word she's sayin'."

"That must be Margaret. Oh, how nice," she said as she took the receiver from Glen. "Hello, this is Patti."

"Oh, Patti, this is Margaret Overstreet from Sudbury. Do you remember me?"

"Of course, Margaret. How are you and where are you?"

"I'm just ducky. Stayin' with me cousin in Bay Village. Is that near you, dear?"

"It's about fifteen miles west of here, not a bad drive. You can get on Interstate Ninety and be here in no time. Why don't you bring your cousin and come for dinner tomorrow night."

"Oh, that would be just ducky. Can hardly wait to see your wee one. Was it a boy or girl?"

"Margaret," her voice cracking, "My baby girl only lived four days. She had a lot of problems. I'll tell you all about it when you get here."

"Oh, swee'heart. I'm so sorry for 'ya. You must be heartbroken. And your dear husband, is he helpin' ya through it?"

"That's another story, too, Margaret. Listen, we'll see you at six. I'll put Dad on and let him give you directions."

"Toodleoo, dear. See you tomorrow, we will."

She let Glen finish the conversation as she went in and dropped on the sofa. "Now I'll have to go all over this again. Maybe it'll help and I'd sure rather be giving her the truth than let people make up their own story."

Margaret's cousin, Penelope O'Dwyer, found the house with no trouble. She had married a man from Cleveland and moved here ten years ago. Her accent moved, too. She was still as hard to understand at times as Margaret. They were a jolly twosome, so much like Cynthia and Margaret. After one of Helen's roast beef dinners with lemon meringue pie for dessert, they all settled in the living room and Patti showed them pictures of her wedding and of Rose. They oohed and aahed at the wedding pictures and cried as Patti told them about Rose's birth and death.

"Oh, such a pity. She was a beautiful wee one, she was," Margaret sobbed. "And I'm so sorry to hear about your..." she hesitated, "... divorce. Would 'ya be mindin' if I tell the good father about your troubles? He always seemed to be so fond of 'ya."

"I suppose that would be okay. How is he?"

"Oh, he's been wearin' a long face, he has. Cynthia and I think he's needin' a wife. Such a nice man, he is. We heard he might be leavin' the church."

"You mean St. Mary's or leaving the clergy?" Patti asked in astonishment.

"Oh, we think it's just St. Mary's. Someone came 'round the store last week and said they was lookin' for a temporary rector. I don't know, maybe he's been feeling bad... or just missin' some people," she said with a cool grin and a twinkle in her eye.

Patti hugged Margaret as they left and promised to come back to Sudbury someday.

"Those were sure nice ladies, but darned if I could understand 'em," Glen laughed. "They sure talk funny."

"Dad, we sound the same way to them."

Helen, listening in to this conversation, came out of the kitchen.

"What would she have been referring to when she said the rector was missing *some people*. Have some of his parishioners disappeared?"

"Gee, Mom, I don't know what she meant by that."

Margaret shared all the news about Patti with Cynthia... embellishing a bit here and there. In short time Sudbury and Kersey townfolk... including Father Beacham, were also aware of what had happened to *that sweet Mrs. North.*

****

The divorce proceedings were handled swiftly, for which Patti was grateful. Edward Laing, at her request, did not insist on an unusually large settlement, though she was deserving of much more. Due to the notoriety of William's recent charges and the famous North name, the courtroom was full of reporters and people who were inquisitive. As Patti looked around the old paneled room, she saw a very familiar face...Paula Stratamondi. "Wonder if she's here out of curiosity or waiting to pounce on the eligible bachelor?" Her flaming red hair was piled high on her head and the revealing dress she wore left little to imagine about her assets. "Guess he won't have much trouble finding consolation for his hurt ego and his thinner wallet."

The case did not require a jury. Edward had seen that it was placed on the docket to go in front of a judge he could trust… not the one from the recent trial. Money and political friendships were evident in the outcome there, and "I won't let you get that same unfair treatment, Patti," he assured her at their first meeting to go over details. She liked his gentlemanly, yet professional manner, and felt total trust with him, just as she had with Tyler Ford.

Two months had passed since the divorce was final and it had been four months since Rose died. It was time to *get on with it* as her friends in Kersey would say. She kept busy responding to advertisements in the newspaper and accepted several appointments for interviews. Though she had no desire to get back into the art business, afraid her path would cross with Norths, she tried to seek out some way she could use her art experience without being involved with galleries.

Offered a position with a florist… it was creative… she accepted and tried to find energy and enthusiasm to carry on. Her duties would include working with corporate accounts on their weekly orders. She would have the opportunity to suggest colors, types of flowers and styles of arrangements for offices and lobbies. It wasn't what she really wanted, but the pay was decent and the company was only three miles from the house. "It will do until… whatever."

Days ran into other days and Patti tried to find contentment. The customers liked her and commented on her happy personality. Little did they know what was under the facade of the smile.

Two months into her new job, she was sitting at the front counter checking client appointments when she heard the little bells ring as the glass front door opened. The tall, blond man in the grey suit with the clerical collar reached his hand toward her.

"Patti, I've come to take you home… to Kersey."

Carol Sue Ravenel

AFTERWORD

The wedding of Patti Hopkins North and Father Nigel Thomas Beacham took place at St. Mary's Church, Kersey, the Saturday after Easter. Tom's friend, Father Peter Clark Phillips, the rector at Holy Trinity in Long Medford, performed the service. In attendance were Helen and Glen Mead who flew over from Cleveland to share Patti's happy day. They stayed in the cottage. Colin Wadsworth took the train from London and brought greetings from his staff at the Tramore. Priscilla and Charles Abbott arranged the reception, with the help of Cynthia Stiles and Margaret Overstreet, who acted like mothers-of-the-bride. Rosie and Paddy Houlehan supplied the food and beverages, Rosie wearing a new dress that Cynthia and Margaret said *was her.* Robert Barrow and his wife closed the pottery for the day to attend the wedding and Doctors Alan Tolbert and Andrew Burton canceled their usual golf date to be there. John Dunthorne wore his best suit for the occasion. Harriett and Richard Olmsted drove up from London. They stayed with friends in Sudbury, as the big house and cottage now had new owners. They had sold it to the rector.

The population of Kersey increased by four the next ten years as the Beacham family grew to include two boys and twin girls. The big house was always full of laughter, and an occasional tear. Patti's life from Cinderella to simple suited her just fine as she found her peace in Kersey. The cottage garden flourished and was enjoyed by the subsequent cottage tenants who shared the Beacham yard with its children and pets. There were always roses in the garden... in memory of one Rose.

Printed in the United States
6395